The Emancipation of WILLIAM JONES, JR.

The Emancipation of William Jones, Jr.
Copyright © 2024 by Judith A. Perkins

Published in the United States of America

Library of Congress Control Number: 2024913256
ISBN   Paperback: 979-8-89091-614-3
ISBN   eBook: 979-8-89091-615-0

All rights reserved. No part of this publication may be reproduced, stored in a retrieval system or transmitted in any way by any means, electronic, mechanical, photocopy, recording or otherwise without the prior permission of the author except as provided by USA copyright law.

The opinions expressed by the author are not necessarily those of ReadersMagnet, LLC.

ReadersMagnet, LLC
10620 Treena Street, Suite 230
San Diego, California, 92131 USA
1.619. 354. 2643 | www.readersmagnet.com

Book design copyright © 2024 by ReadersMagnet, LLC. All rights reserved.

Cover design by Tifanny Curaza
Interior design by Don De Guzman

The *Emancipation* of WILLIAM JONES, JR.

JUDITH A. PERKINS

Chapter 1

"You will eat your breakfast, then you will go to school. There will be no further discussion," ordered Anna.

Six-year-old William looked up at his mama with sad eyes. "I cannot eat anymore mama, I'm full," he said.

"I bought that food for you, and you will eat it!" she commanded.

William sat at the table with tears running down his dirty face. He was a small boy with big, sad blue eyes. "Okay, Mama, I will try." William was afraid to disobey his mother for fear of being hit.

"I am not made of money, William. Do you think I like having to spend money on you?" she growled, which caused more tears to run down William's face. "Stop your sniveling! You'll be late for school. I need to get some more sleep before I have to go to work."

William managed to finish his breakfast, put his coat on, and leave before his mama got mad at him again. On the way to school, he stepped into some bushes and threw up most of his breakfast.

Anna left the dishes for William to clean up when he got home from school. She went back to bed and slept for several hours before she had to get ready for work at the tavern down the street.

Anna was a good-looking girl. She had long brown hair that she wore in a bun at the nape of her neck. She had the best clothes that she could possibly afford. Most of her paychecks went for clothing and accessories for her own use. She spent and gave very little to William, including her time.

Anna and William lived in Lewiston, Idaho. She was a 24-year-old widow trying to raise her son. She never wanted a child and had never bonded with William. Her parents had forced her to take care of him when he was a baby. She did take care of him but found no joy in it.

In 1901, she and William moved to Lewiston from Rawlings, WA where her parents owned the hotel and restaurant. She had three sisters and one brother and did not get along with any of them. She was the oldest and from the time they were born, she resented them. She felt she should have had all the attention from her parents, grandmother, and aunts.

Anna wanted her freedom but was still responsible for William. She did as little as possible to take care of him now. She did just enough to stay out of trouble with the school and the law. Anna worked until after midnight six days a week and if she had a date, many times would not get home until early in the morning. William was alone most of that time. There was a lady in the building they lived in who would look in on William once in a while, but she was gone a lot of the time also.

William was a smart child but did not know how to apply that intelligence. Anna spent very little money on him and therefore, his clothes were often ragged and dirty. He tried to wash his own clothes but didn't do a very good job.

Usually, breakfast was the only meal he ate during the day. His mother worked at night, and there was no food that he was able to prepare himself.

William did not attend school. His mother did not know he was not going when he left the house in the morning. He would throw up his breakfast, then find a place to sit where no one would notice him or no one would care if he was there.

In August 1905, Anna decided to take William to Rawlings for a visit. She wanted to see her family. She wrote her father a letter asking him to buy them a train ticket. She wanted William to see his grandparents, aunts, and uncles. She told her father that she missed them. George was suspicious of her reasons, but he bought William and Anna the ticket anyway. He wanted to see his grandson.

Anna arrived with William and most of his clothing. When asked why she brought so much, she said that he got dirty so fast, he had to change his clothes several times a day.

Anna stayed at the hotel, but William stayed with his grandparents in their home. There were two trains a day to Lewiston. After Anna and William were there for three days, Anna boarded the evening train without her family knowing it and went back to Lewiston without William.

When George found out what she had done, he broke down and cried. He wondered what had happened to his beautiful first-born child.

William did not seem to be overly upset about his mother leaving without him. He was happy having someone to pay attention to him. He loved being tucked into bed each night and not having to find something to eat himself. He was allowed to eat the amount that he could and was not forced to overeat.

William was not used to having a man around all of the time. George was kind and loving to him, but William was suspicious of the attention. The only male contact he had were his mama's occasional boyfriends and they were not very nice to him. They would either ignore him or close him in a closet while they were visiting his mother.

Marie was baffled at the dinner table when William did not dish up his own food. Anna had allotted him only so much food. He was forced to eat all that he was given. Sometimes that was more than he could eat and sometimes he went hungry because his mother forgot to buy enough food for him.

"William, why aren't you taking any food? Aren't you hungry?" asked Marie.

"I am not allowed, ma'am," answered William.

"What do you mean, 'not allowed'? asked Marie.

"My mama won't let me dish up my own food. She said that sometimes there wasn't enough for me, so she dished it up herself," commented William.

"Well, here you can dish up your own food William and have as much as you want. We always have enough food here. Your Grandpa is a very good cook," said Marie.

"Thank you, ma'am," answered William.

"William, you can call me Grandma if you want," said Marie. William nodded and dished up some food on his plate. He ate what he had dished up, looking up at Marie several times like he was waiting to be punished for something.

When he finished his food, he sat at the table with his hands in his lap. He said nothing to Marie and sat there with his head down. Marie was confused with his demeanor and looked at George with a questioning look.

"William, would you like to go for a walk with me?" asked George.

"Yes sir. That would be okay," answered William.

"Excuse me ma'am," said William as he left with George.

Marie was baffled by William's attitude towards her. It was almost like he was afraid of her. She wondered if he was afraid of Anna. What in the world had her daughter done to this precious little boy?

William walked with George around the town. George stopped in at Clyde's general store. James was working at the store and greeted George as he came in. "Who do you have there Mr. Seevers?" asked James.

"This is my grandson, William Jones," answered George. "William, this is James Kingman. He works for Clyde Rodgers, the owner of the store." "James, we are here for a piece of candy. I thought that would top off our meal nicely."

"I can't have candy," said William.

"Why not?" asked George.

"Mama says I'm not good enough for candy," Will answered.

George looked at Clyde with anger in his eyes. "Well, William, I say you are good enough for two pieces of candy," answered George.

Anna Seevers Jones was living in a rooming house in Lewiston, Idaho and working in the Lucky Lady Saloon down the street. The saloon closed at 2:00 A.M. and she had to clean up after the last customer left, which usually got her home about 3:00 A.M. Sometimes she took a customer home with her, but most of the time she was too tired after an evening of getting drinks for a bunch of drunk patrons.

She really wanted to get a job in an upscale lounge. She had to save enough money to move out of the crummy place she was living in and buy some decent clothes to wear to interview for a job at one of the better saloons. She thought that she could be one of the servers or even one of the dancers. She would make a killing on tips if she could work there.

Anna felt that one of the smartest things she did was leave William in Rawlings with her parents. He was such a bother to have around and was an extra expense she did not need. He had never fit into her plans for her future.

Anna had never wanted to have children and she was very angry when she found out she was pregnant. Her husband Will had been a crew member of a cargo ship that sunk in a typhoon in the China Sea in April 1895. She was seven months pregnant when she received word of his ship going down. She was angry at Will for telling her that he would be back in 3 months when it could be at least a year before he was back.

She would not have had the baby if she had known he wouldn't be back when he said he would. She never wanted children and thought it was stupid every time one of her aunts had a baby when she lived at home. She couldn't wait to get away from her home and her parents. All the time she was growing up, she felt she should have been the only child. She resented her sisters and her brother for interfering with what she wanted in life and taking her parents' attention away from her.

At least she did not have to think about William now. Her parents could have him.

Anna dressed in her finest dress one afternoon and went uptown to an upscale hotel to apply for a job in their bar. Since she was raised in a hotel, she thought that it might give her an edge in getting the job. She was a good bartender and could pour almost any type of drink. Even though there was no bar in her father's hotel in Rawlings, she watched and learned from every bar she went into. She would sit at the bar and listen and watch the bartender as he mixed the drinks. She also noticed how much the bartender made in tips.

Joe Archer was the manager of the bar in the Lewiston Arms Hotel. He was badly in need of another waitress to help with the evening crowd.

When Anna came up to the bar at two o'clock in the afternoon asking to apply for the job, he was intrigued. "Would you mind waiting for 15 minutes? My afternoon replacement is due in, and I will have some time to talk to you. Have a seat. Would you like something to drink?" Joe asked Anna. "A cup of tea would be nice," Anna asked nervously.

Anna sat at a small round table to the side of the bar where she could see what Mr. Archer was doing behind the bar. He set a cup of tea down in front of her along with sugar and cream and let her know he would be with her in a few minutes.

Twenty-five minutes later, Joe Archer finally sat down at the table with Anna. He apologized for the delay. His replacement was late for work again.

"Well Miss Jones, what makes you want to work in a place like this?" asked Joe. "First of all, I am Mrs. Jones. I am a widow and have been for 8 years. I was raised in a hotel in Rawlings, Washington and know the hotel business fairly well. There was no bar in the hotel, but I have been bartending for the past 8 years to support myself and my son," explained Anna.

"If you have a child, who takes care of him while you are working? One of the problems I am having now is with a working mother who does not have reliable childcare and cannot always get to work on time. Then when the child is sick, she can't come at all," asked Joe.

'My son is living with his grandparents in Rawlings and will not be a concern," explained Anna.

"Are you working now Anna?" asked Joe. Anna decided to be completely honest with Joe and answered, "Yes, I am working at The Lucky Lady Saloon down by the river. It is not the best place to work, but it was all I could get at the time I moved here. It is not easy for a woman with a child to find a job.

"I will give you a chance at the job, Anna. Report here for work tomorrow at two o'clock in the afternoon. You will be working until 11:00 in the evening. I will work the closing shift until 2:00 AM. Please wear a black skirt and a white blouse and I will give you an apron to wear. It will be your responsibility to keep the apron clean. You will only be issued one apron. If you need more, the cost will come out of your pay. You will be paid $6.00 per week plus half of the tips you make. I will expect you to be at work and ready to start on time."

"Thank you, Mr. Archer. I will be on time and ready to start work. Will there be someone here to show me where things are and the procedures you have?" asked Anna.

"Yes, I will be here for your first shift, then you will be on your own. Also, please call me Joe."

Anna had to rush out and see if she could find herself a black skirt before tomorrow. She had a white blouse, but no black skirt. She just hoped that she had enough money to buy the skirt. She went to the local mercantile to see what they had. They did have a black skirt in her size for $1.50. She only had $5.00 to her name and had to have trolley fare to get home after work in the evening. She knew she had to be in her room at the boarding house for at least another month until she got a paycheck and could move to something closer.

Anna purchased the skirt, then decided to save the trolley money and walk home. It was still early enough and light enough outside for her to walk safely.

She worked her shift at the saloon that evening, but let the owner know that it would be her last night. She was moving on. He was not happy about Anna's decision and tried to talk her out of it, Even offering her five cents more per hour if she would stay. She declined, finished her shift, and went home Relieved not to have to go back to that dump again. Soon she would be able to move out of this boarding house into something much nicer and closer to her new job.

CHAPTER 2

Bill Kingman and Valerie Seevers finished school at the same time even though Bill was three years older than Valerie. They had been seeing each other since they graduated, and Bill had finally asked her father for her hand in marriage. A June 1906 wedding was being planned.

Bill's mother Virginia had married Clyde Rodgers Jr. after her divorce from Otis Kingman. Otis was confined in the Walla Walla State Prison for manslaughter, child endangerment and spousal abuse. His original three-year sentence was extended to twenty years because of fighting and causing the death of another prisoner. Fighting was Otis' way of settling arguments and he was in solitary confinement much of the time. His first parole hearing was in two months and unless he changed his ways, he would not be paroled. Virginia and her children were always on alert for fear Otis would get out and come after them. He had never believed that she divorced him and still considered her his wife. He had threatened her and their children several times, even though he was in prison.

She and Clyde were very happy together. Clyde doted on her and loved all of her children and they in turned thought the world of Clyde just for the fact that he made their mother happy.

Bill and Valerie were excited about getting married. Bill was saving every bit of his salary from working at the JSJ Ranch. He lived in the bunkhouse and had very few expenses. He had a good down payment saved for a farm of his own. He and Valerie had found the perfect place two miles outside of town. It was a 100-acre farm with a good house, barn, and other outbuildings on the property. Jeff and Susan Jordan gave them a good reference at the bank for a loan and with Bill's substantial down payment, the monthly payments would not be beyond their reach.

There were some repairs that needed to be done to the house, but they had plenty of time to get them done. Valerie wanted their home to always be some place bright, cheerful, and comfortable for Bill to come home to. He grew up in a house that was always dingy and dirty. His mother tried to keep it clean, but Bill's father never cared and was always tracking dirt into the house and laughing about it. He was mean and nasty to his children, often beating them for no apparent reason and depriving them of food.

Bill was so sweet and kind. He was totally different from his father and Valerie was completely and totally in love with him.

Virginia was very proud of all of her children. Her two oldest sons, Seth and Daniel worked for JSJ Ranch and were likely to stay there. They were both trusted employees, doing whatever task was assigned to them.

Bill and Valerie were planning their future together and Josephine was in nursing school in Walla Walla. She had another year of study and would probably look for a job in a hospital when she finished.

James was working with Clyde in the general store. He was preparing to take over when Clyde decided to retire.

Margaret, or Maggie as everyone called her, was still in school and living at home with Clyde and Virginia. She helped her mother in the housekeeping department at the hotel in her spare time.

Even though the three older boys got a late start in school, all of Virginia's children were very intelligent and were great kids.

Virginia just hoped that Otis would not get out of prison and try to get in touch with any of the children. She feared for their lives if he did.

George and Marie Seevers were trying very hard to integrate their grandson William into the family. He was a 10-year-old boy who had no confidence in himself. His mother had made all of his decisions for him.

When Anna left him in Rawlings with them, he only had one change of clothes and one pair of shoes that had holes in them. His coat was thin and threadbare. It was obvious that Anna spent very little time or money on him.

They were stunned at Anna's treatment of William and were saddened when she abandoned him, but felt it was their obligation to look after him even though it would put a strain on their health. They had worked long, hard hours most of their married life and were tired and ready for their son Freddie to take over the hotel and restaurant. They both wanted to retire to Cannon Beach, Oregon.

With both Isaac and John Taylor at school in the east, Steven and Jane offered to have William live with them. They had the extra room and were anxious to have another child around the house. George and Marie loved their grandson dearly but were relieved when Steven and Jane made the offer.

George, Marie, Steven, and Jane all tried to prepare William for another move. They wanted him to understand that his grandparents loved him and were not abandoning him, but he had more room at his Aunt Jane's house. They all assured William that he was welcome to come to the hotel or to his grandparents' house anytime he wanted.

"Why doesn't my Mama want me?" asked William.

The four adults sat and looked at him in stunned silence. Steven answered, "We don't know, William. Maybe something happened a long time ago. I'm sure she wants you but feels you will have a better life living here with your whole family. We all want you here in Rawlings with us and we all love you. You will be living here with your Aunt Jane and me, but that does not mean you cannot visit anyone of your family anytime you want to. There are a lot of aunts and uncles and cousins to get to know. Soon Aunt Valerie will get married, and you will have more family."

"Will they still want me then?" asked William.

"They sure will!" said Grandpa George and gave William a hug around the shoulders. With the hug, William stiffened and moved away slightly.

"I think it would be a good idea to talk to Aunt Susan and Uncle Jeff and see if we can all go out there soon for a big family dinner. Maybe Uncle Jeff will teach you to ride a horse," added Grandma Marie.

"I would not know what to say around all of those people. Mama never wanted me to talk when there were a lot of people around. She said that it took the attention away from her. She would get really mad when anyone would ask me a question. She always made me leave the room."

"William, we will never stop you from speaking. When you want to ask a question or make a statement, you may do so. You will be included in any conversation," Marie emphasized.

"If we are speaking privately with someone, we will go to another room, not make you leave," said George. "Anyway, your Mama isn't here and even if she was, I would not let her touch you in anger."

The next day, Jane contacted Susan about having a family dinner at the ranch. She explained William's fear and apprehension to Susan. "He is scared to death to be around adults. And according to Irene, he was scared to be around the kids in school also. I think Anna beat him and would not allow him to speak when he was around adults," explained Jane.

"It looks like we have our work cut out for us. Our job now is to first, make him feel safe and then to help him build some self-confidence," Susan commented.

Irene Seevers was 27 years old and was the school teacher in Rawlings, Washington. Irene was raised in Rawlings, but when she graduated from high school and obtained her teaching certificate from the state of Washington, she took a position in Colfax, Washington.

When Fiona Stephens decided to retire from teaching school and spend time with her husband, Dr. Blake Stephens, Irene jumped at the chance to move home and be the teacher in Rawlings. She loved the idea of being close to her family.

The town had financed a second story apartment on the school building as an incentive to attract a new teacher. It would be a great place for Irene to live. She did not want to move back in with her parents since she had been away so long.

Irene loved to cook and had become quite good at it. She was anxious to have a kitchen of her own to be able to experiment with her recipes.

Marie and Jane went to see Irene the week before school started to talk about William. They were concerned about his lack of self-confidence and lack of social skills.

They could find no record of attendance at the school in Lewiston. Irene did not know what grade level to place him in. None of them had any idea of his reading or math skills.

"I haven't seen him pick up a book to read since he's been here," said Marie. "I don't know if he knows how to read."

Irene explained to the two women, "He should be in the fifth grade according to his age level, but I doubt if he can do fifth grade level work."

"I really doubt if Anna took much interest in his schooling," Marie said sadly.

"I'll work with him as much as possible and assess his abilities to see what curriculum he needs. I don't want him to feel different or backwards in any way," Irene emphasized.

"I agree!" said Marie. "We must go and let Irene get back to work."

"Thanks, you two, for filling me in. William's presence in the classroom will make for an interesting year," mused Irene.

After Marie and Jane left, Irene sat at her desk wondering what happened to Anna and why she had such a negative attitude towards her son. She and Anna were never close growing up, but they were raised by the same loving parents who treated all of their children equally and gave them all their love and attention. There seemed to be something lacking in Anna and it was a puzzle to know what or why.

William moved from his grandparents' home to his Uncle William and Aunt Jane's home. He had a bedroom of his own but was encouraged to join the family as much as possible. After supper, they played games, sang songs, read stories, or just talked to each other. They called it family time.

When asked to read a story, William declined and asked to be excused to his room, saying he was tired and wanted to go to bed early. Steven excused him reluctantly, thinking that maybe the change in location was concerning him. School started the next day and maybe he wanted to be well rested for his first day.

William wasn't tired, he was just scared. He was afraid to go to school the next day. He just knew everyone was going to laugh at him because he didn't know how to read and didn't know his numbers very well. His Mama didn't like him to read. She said it reminded her too much of when she was little, and everyone had their nose in a book and were not paying any attention to her. William always tried to do what his Mama told him too. She would hit him if he didn't.

William slept fitfully and woke up sick to his stomach. He didn't want any breakfast but ate something anyway. He figured he would find some bushes on the way to school and throw up in them. Then he would go someplace and hide for the day, but Aunt Jane said that she had to go to the store and the school was on the way, so she would walk with him. He couldn't figure out a way to get out of going.

When they reached the school, Jane hollered a greeting to Irene and said goodbye to William and went on to the store. Irene greeted William with a handshake, welcomed him to the class and continued to greet the other students as they came in the door. She instructed the students to find their names on the desks and have a seat. William looked at her in fear but continued into the room. He knew what his name looked like, and after a time found his desk.

William's fear was evident to Irene. Something had happened to him at his school in Lewiston and she was determined to find out. She would write to the school and request his records. She needed them to determine what grade level he was and what his test scores were.

In the meantime, she would do what she could to help him to socialize and be comfortable in her classroom.

"Good morning class! Welcome to the Rawlings School. My name is Miss Seevers. I am new to this school as a teacher, but I went to school here as a child. I graduated from this school and went to Colfax to teach for several years. When Mrs. Stephen's retired, I came back to teach. I am excited to be back in my hometown and be able to be your teacher."

"Not only am I new to this school as a teacher, but we also have two new students to our school and our town. The first student is Jennifer Abbott who has moved here from Butte, Montana. Jennifer is in the second grade.

Our second new student is William Jones. William has moved here from Lewiston, Idaho and will be in the fourth grade. Let's all welcome these new students to Rawlings and to our school" said Irene as she and the class clapped for them. Jennifer looked eager to get started and William cowered in his seat and looked terrified.

The day went fairly well for Irene, but she feared not as well for William. He raced out of the classroom at the end of the day and started running in the opposite direction of Steven and Jane's house.

Irene saw him running and called after him, but he either did not hear her or ignored her. She quickly closed up the school and went to Jane's house. Steven was home working on some papers. When he heard what had happened, he got in his buggy and went after William.

Jane was distraught at William's actions. "Irene, he never talks to us. He is always very polite at the dinner table. He takes his plates to the sink and even washes them. He keeps his room clean and tidy, but he doesn't play or laugh or talk at all. Steven offered to toss a ball back and forth with him last night, but he said he was tired and went to his room. He will answer questions with one word answers and says, "yes sir" and "no sir", but never says more. He does not interact with anyone."

Steven came back to the house with William cowering by his side in the buggy. They got down when Jane ran out of the house towards William to give him a hug. William recoiled and covered his head like he was going to be hit.

Jane stopped suddenly and looked at William, then at Steven. "He said he was going to go back to Lewiston and his Mama," explained Steven.

"At least she let me do what I wanted and didn't care as long as I didn't bother her," cried William.

"She never checked if I was in school or not. She always went back to bed."

"Were you ever in school William?" asked Irene.

"No. I didn't go at all. She didn't care and I don't understand why you do," cried William.

"We love you William and we want you to have the best life you can have," said Jane. "You are a special person in our lives and we want you to be happy."

"Were you often hungry, William?" asked Irene.

"Not in the morning. Mama would make me a big breakfast and make me eat it all. She said that she didn't go to all that work to throw the food away. When I left to go to school, I would go into the bushes and throw it up," explained William.

"What did you eat for supper?" Steven asked.

"Nothing! Mama wasn't home. She was at work, and she didn't want me to mess up the house. She said I only needed one meal a day anyway," said William.

Steven, Jane, and Irene sat there stunned at what William said. Jane reassured William that he would not go hungry, nor would he be forced to eat more than he wanted.

They also assured him that they all loved him, that he was family. William looked at them with a blank look when they mentioned the word "love".

After they talked to him for a few more minutes, he asked to be excused. They all nodded, and he went to his room.

"I don't think that boy knows what "love" is." Steven said. "Have you noticed how he stiffens every time someone touches him or tries to hug him? I'll bet you Anna never gave him any love at all."

"Mama told me that when William was born, Anna wanted nothing to do with him. Mama had to force her to take care of him. Apparently, she resented it," explained Irene. "She would leave him in a wet or dirty diaper because she thought it was nasty to have to change him."

"Mama said she never did see her cuddle him," added Irene.

"Let's talk to Susan and Jeff about this. Somehow, we have to instill in William the idea of being loved and loving someone else." Steven emphasized.

William sat in his room thinking about his family. They said they loved him, but he didn't know what that meant. None of them were mean to him or hit him like his mama did. They didn't make him do chores and if they did ask him to do something, they always said please and thank you. And they smiled at him. He liked the way it made him feel when they smiled at him. Mama never smiled at him.

He didn't like the hugs though. He wasn't used to getting hugs. When one of mama's boyfriends hugged him, it was usually because he was mad, or he wanted him to go away for a while. They would always hug too hard, and it hurt.

He sat in his room for a while when Jane came and told him that supper was ready. He went to the kitchen, washed his hands, and sat down with his hands in his lap.

Steven put out his hand to William to hold it. He watched his aunt Jane hold Steven's other hand, so he put his hand up and into Steven's hand. Steven said a short prayer and then they passed the dishes. William wasn't sure what to do, so he just passed the dish onto Aunt Jane without dishing anything onto his plate. He did that with two dishes when Jane asked him if he was hungry.

"Yes ma'am," William answered.

"Then why didn't you dish any food onto your plate?" asked Jane.

William answered with tears in his eyes, "Mama said that I was never to take the food myself. If I was allowed to eat supper, she would dish it up for me.

"William, in this house, you are welcome to dish up your own food. If you want more, you can help yourself. You take as much as you think you can eat. If you do not like something, let me know. I am not the good cook that your Grandpa George is, but I can put together a fairly good meal," explained Jane.

William was hesitant about dishing up his own food, so he only took a little of every dish on the table. There was a dish of applesauce to go along with the pork roast that Jane had made. William tried a little bit of the applesauce and his eyes got big. "I like this. What is it?" asked William.

"It is applesauce made from the apples down by the hotel. Your Grandma, Aunts and I made the sauce last fall when the apples were ripe," explained Jane.

"It is very good. I like the taste of sweet things," said William.

"I do too!" exclaimed Steven and laughed.

"William, have you ever eaten a piece of fresh fruit that was not out of a can?" asked Jane.

"I don't think so. Mama didn't buy stuff like that for me. I saw her one time eating a piece of something she called a plum, but she said I couldn't have any."

Jane got up from the table and went to the counter and picked up a fresh plum that came from the tree in their yard. "Here, try this. It is a plum," said Jane. William took it with wide eyes. He looked at Jane, then at Steven like he was questioning whether he really could have it.

"Go ahead, taste it," said Steven.

William bit into the plum and immediately had juice running down his chin and onto his shirt. He looked down at his shirt and got a horrified, scared look on his face. "I will wash my shirt and get the stains out," he said as he put the plum down on his plate. He started to get up, but Jane stopped him with a hand on his shoulder.

"It's okay William. You do not have to wash your own shirt and I do not mind if you have plum juice on your shirt. Do you like the taste of the plum?"

"Oh yes," replied William. "It is probably the best thing I have ever tasted."

"That plum came from a tree in our back yard. You may go out to the tree and pick a plum to eat anytime you feel like it. We have more than we can use, and you are welcome to eat them. Just be careful. If you eat too many of them, they might upset your stomach and you will be spending a lot of time in the outhouse," Steven said with a laugh in his voice.

"You probably should finish some more of your supper before you fill up on plums," Jane mentioned. William got busy and ate almost all of what was on his plate. He said that he wanted to save some space for another plum and asked to be excused from the table. He took his dishes to the sink and started to wash them, but Jane stopped him. "William, you do not have to wash your own dishes. I will do all of them and clean up the kitchen. You go out and get yourself another plum."

"I will go with you, William. It is necessary to pick a ripe plum. I will show you how to choose a ripe one," said Steven as he led him out of the kitchen to the back yard and the all-important plum tree.

The next morning, poor William was in absolute misery with a crampy stomach and bowels. Jane asked him how many plums he had eaten the night before and William told her he had eaten a lot of them. "No wonder you are feeling awful. You stay close to the outhouse today. You will need it. Please do not worry William, neither Steven nor I are mad at you. We are sorry you do not feel well."

William did love those plums but learned his lesson. He would not eat as many next time.

Chapter 3

Electricity was established in Rawlings in 1899 with the railroad depot being the first building to have electricity installed. George Seevers decided that the hotel would be the second building to be electrified.

In 1893, telephone service was established in Spokane, but it wasn't until 1904 that the city of Rawlings decided it was time to bring it to their town. The town was becoming a modern city.

The main switchboard was installed in the hotel. There was a separate room behind the post office that was used for the equipment. The town council hired a woman who had lived in Rawlings for three years to be the switchboard operator. She was Stella Monroe and was a widow. Her husband was killed in a farming accident in Idaho a year before she moved to Rawlings. She had a small savings at the bank, and was able to live on it, but wanted something to do in her spare time. Stella lived in a small house just a short distance from the hotel, so it was easy for her to walk to work.

Stella had quickly learned the ins and outs of running the switchboard and became very adept at operating it.

Clyde had a telephone put in the general store. And one was installed in the bank and in the sheriff's office. And of course, the railroad depot had telephone service, along with the telegraph.

The idea of the general population having a phone in their homes was a little foreign to the citizens, but they finally realized that they could not contact any of the businesses without one, so slowly, the families had phones installed.

Stella was working long hours and finally decided that she had to train someone else to help her. She talked to Irene Seevers, the schoolteacher, to see if there was a young lady who would like to work part-time after school.

Irene knew of just the young lady who could do the job. She was 16 years old and would graduate from high school in June. She could not afford to go on to school and was not interested in being a farmer's wife. Her name was Mary Allen. She lived with her widowed mother in a house on the edge of town. Her father had been older and had been very ill for a long time. Mary's mother had cared for him until he died 3 months ago. They could certainly use the extra income, even though it would not be much.

Mary went into the hotel and asked for Stella at the main desk. She was directed to the switchboard room. As she went back to the room, she became very nervous. She had never interviewed for a job before, and she wanted the job very much. There was not much else available in Rawlings, and she could not leave her mother to find work in another city.

Stella greeted Mary with a big smile and immediately put Mary at ease. "Would you have any problems working in the evenings or on the weekend?" asked Stella.

"No maam, I wouldn't. There is only my mother and me and she is very capable of being on her own for a while. She reads and does a lot of her baking at night when the house is cooler.

Stella was interrupted several times during her talk with Mary by the switchboard coming to life and having to make or receive a call. Mary watched very carefully what Stella was doing and was very quick at grasping the idea of incoming and outgoing calls and how to make them. When Stella was done with one call, Mary asked her a couple of questions about the procedure she used, and Stella was very impressed at the degree of knowledge she had in such a short time.

After a few more questions and a few more calls, Stella hired Mary on the spot. She told her about the hours she would be working, and about the salary and most importantly, about the privacy of the phone conversations and about how unethical it was to listen in on anyone's conversation unless she was asked to.

Mary thanked her profusely and left the hotel with a spring in her step. She almost skipped home to tell her mother that she had the job. There was a celebration in the Allen household that evening.

On Saturday afternoon, September 16, 1905, the Seevers, Lewis, Taylor and Jordan families all met at the JSJ Ranch for a big family dinner. There, William was introduced to what a family dinner was like. They were a noisy, happy group of people who all loved and respected each other.

William was a little overwhelmed by all of the attention he was getting. He was also a little overwhelmed at the amount of food that was set on the table. A long table was set up outside and steaks were cooked on an open flame. The weather was perfect to eat outside.

After a while, Earl Jansen, the JSJ Ranch foreman came up to William and gave him a large box and asked him to open it. William had never been given a present before and was a little intimidated by the crowd of people watching him. Uncle Jeff asked him to open the box. William hesitated for a minute longer then opened the lid of the box. Inside was a solid black puppy with a spot of white over one eye like an eye-patch.

The minute the lid was off of the box, the puppy jumped up and licked William's face. William was horrified, fearing someone would think he did something wrong. Everyone laughed. "You can take him out of the box William," said Earl. He is a 'welcome to the family' present to you from your family."

"His name is Patch. His mama and papa live here on the ranch, and he is nine weeks old. He has three brothers and one sister, but they all have homes already. Patch is the last puppy and really needs a boy to take care of him and give him a lot of love and attention."

"You mean this is my puppy?" William said in wonder. "He sure is, if you want him," replied Jeff. All William could say was "OH, OH, OH!" Then he looked at Steven and Jane and asked, "Is it okay if I take him home." "Absolutely!" Steven said. "He belongs to you so where you go, he goes too."

For the rest of the afternoon, William and Patch played until Patch was so tired that he plopped down and promptly went to sleep. William was just about as tired as the puppy but was afraid to take his eyes off of Patch. He was afraid someone would take him away.

While William was out in the field playing with Patch, the adults discussed what to do about William's educational needs.

It was decided that Irene and Susan together would formulate a curriculum that would give him what he needed to learn to read, write and do basic numbers. They all thought it was a good idea to keep him out of the classroom until he could do some basic reading. Jane would work with him at home for a while until he learned to read. If he went into the classroom now, he would be at a complete disadvantage and Irene did not have the time in the classroom to devote to him completely nor did they want him to be ridiculed by the other students. Jane and Susan both were sure that Fiona would be more than happy to help.

The whole family was very pleased to have William living in Rawlings but were baffled at Anna's attitude. They did not know what happened to her and why she was so hard on William.

Hopefully, with Patch in his life now and the rest of the family aware of his situation, he will be able to build some self-confidence and learn to love.

William doted on Patch. He took him everyplace he went. Patch was just as devoted to William. They were inseparable. Steven and Jane looked the other way when Patch decided he didn't like his bed, but liked William's better. They would peek into William's bedroom to check on him and find William and Patch cuddled up next to each other.

George and Marie felt it was time to have a family portrait taken. They had never had one taken of everyone together. They again chose to meet at the Ranch. There was more room for everyone to spread out. Steven and Jane were sorry that their boys were not there. Both of them had jobs for the summer, so chose not to make the long trip home.

Jeff and Susan's son, Jeffrey Jr. was home for a short visit from school in Pullman, WA.

Bill Kingman was there with Valerie Seevers and was included in the photo.

William was sitting on the ground in front of Steven and Jane, and of course, Patch was sitting right next to him.

William had never had his picture taken and was not sure if it was something that was safe to do, but the rest of the family seemed to think it was okay, so he went along.

The camera was very large and was on a stand. The man taking the picture was called a photographer and when he was ready to take it, he put his head under a large piece of cloth. Then he said "ready" and there was a big flash. Patch didn't like that and started to bark.

Everyone assured both Patch and William that it was okay. There had to be a flash to take the picture.

After a lunch of soup and sandwiches that George had brought out from the restaurant, everyone had to leave for home. It was a fun day and William was anxious to see the pictures.

When they reached home, Steven had a message from Stella at the switchboard office. Instead of calling her, he decided to go over to her office. It was right behind the post office, and he had some papers in his office that he wanted to work on at home.

When Steven went into the switchboard office, Stella handed him a folded-up note. "Thanks Stella. I'll read it in my office. I have some papers I want to pick up anyway," he said.

Steven didn't think too much about the note. He often received telephone messages from suppliers asking about orders that he had placed for different clients.

He sat down at his desk, found the papers he wanted and read them over to make sure he knew what he wanted to do. As he was getting up to leave, he remembered the note that Stella had given him.

He opened the note to see who it was from. It was from Anna. She more or less ordered him to call her in Lewiston. The last thing he wanted to do was talk to Anna Jones, but he figured he had better call. It was best to do it here instead of at home where William might hear him.

"Stella, will you please ring the number in Lewiston? And Stella, I am going to ask you to do something that might seem wrong to you, but I have my reasons. Will you please listen in on the call? I would like to have a witness to what I say."

"Yes, I will Steven if you are sure that is what you want. If you would like, I can take notes on the call," suggested Stella.

"That might be a very good idea. Thanks," answered Steven.

Stella rang the number on the note. It was answered by a woman. There was a lot of noise in the background, and it was hard to hear what was said. Steven asked for Anna Jones. The lady on the other end identified herself as Anna Jones. "Anna, this is Steven. You called me. What can I do for you?" he asked.

"I left my son with my parents. What is he doing living with you? I want him back with my parents immediately. And what right did you have to give him a dog without asking my permission first. He does not deserve a dog. He is a willful child and needs to be disciplined, not pampered. And you have exposed him to the whole family."

"Anna, if you stop talking for a minute, I will tell you what we have done. Your parents did not feel that they could adequately take care of a 10-year-old child. Since our boys are away at school, we have the room to have William at our home. As far as the dog is concerned, William was lonesome, and the puppy is very good company for him. Since you have seen fit not to make sure he gets to school every day, he is not able to read. He does not know his letters or numbers. He does not have anything to do during the day, so a puppy is good company for him."

"William went to school every day. I made sure he had a good breakfast and sent him off to school."

"You did not follow up on his attendance. He says he never went. He had to go into the bushes and throw up the breakfast you made him eat because it was too much. He went hungry for the rest of the day because you did not provide any lunch or supper for him," Steven said rather forcefully.

"The little brat. I bought that food, fixed it for him and he threw it up? That little brat. I wasted all that time and money," Anna yelled.

"I want you to put him on the train to Lewiston tomorrow. I do not want you and mousy Jane to raise my child. If my parents do not care enough about their grandchild, then I will see to him myself," demanded Anna.

"No Anna! If you want to talk about William, you come here. We would love to talk to you about William. The whole family has some things we would like to say to you about William," Steven said and then hung up the phone.

Steven sat in his chair with his heart pounding and so mad he was seeing red. Stella came into the office and handed him 2 sheets of paper with notes on them about the phone call with Anna. "Thanks Stella. Please don't say anything about this to anyone. I need to talk to Jane and to the rest of the family," said Steven.

"Of course, I won't say anything. Good luck! She sounds like a difficult person to deal with," emphasized Stella.

"She is," answered Steven. "Is Mary Lou coming in soon?"

"Yes. She should be here anytime now. Try to have a good evening, Steven."

"Thanks, you too," said Steven.

As Steven walked home from his office, he thought about his conversation with Anna and her attitude towards William. Something must have happened to her to make her so abusive and just plain hateful to her own son. He was sure George and Marie were very upset and at a loss as to know why she was the way she was.

Steven knew one thing. He was not going to send William back to Lewiston without a fight. He felt an obligation to take care of William and to see that he had the best life that he could possibly give him. And Patch would be a part of that life.

As Steven was walking home, he was trying to figure out what they were going to do about William. Both he and Jane were becoming very attached to him and loved having him around. He was still hesitant about the hugs and affection shown to him. He had never had any before and did not know how to respond.

Right now, Steven was inclined to get a lawyer and seek temporary custody of William. Obviously, Anna was not capable of taking care of him properly. She worked in the evenings and William was totally alone. A ten-year-old boy needs supervision. He needs friends to play with and he needs his mother to pay attention to him. William would have none of that if he went back to Lewiston.

William was outside tossing a stick to Patch and trying to teach him to fetch it and return it to him. He wasn't having much success, but looked like he was having fun.

Patch saw Steven walking home and ran to him. William did not see Steven and thought Patch was running away. Then he saw Steven bend down to give Patch a rub behind his ears and breathed a sigh of relief.

"Hi William. How are you doing training Patch to fetch?" asked Steven.

"Not very well," answered William. "He just wants to chew on the stick and won't bring it back to me."

"That's pretty normal for a pup Patch's age. He is getting his teeth and wants to chew on everything. It relieves some of the pain of teething. Just keep up the tossing and he will learn to bring it back to you," explained Steven. "Is your Aunt Jane inside the house?"

"Yes sir. She is in there cooking something that smells really good," said William.

Steven walked inside the kitchen and agreed with William. It smelled really good. "Hi sweetheart. I have something I want to talk to you about, but I think we had better include George and Marie in the conversation."

"Does it have to do with William," Jane asked with a concerned look on her face.

"Yes, but I would rather he not hear the conversation now," explained Steven.

The three of them sat down to a meal of Venison Stew made with vegetables from their own garden. William was very impressed that he was eating food that he had helped dig out of the garden.

Patch was learning to sit on his pillow during dinner. If he was good, he would get a treat after dinner. It was almost always a piece of meat. William was very good about not forcing him to eat things he didn't like or want.

After dinner, William took Patch back outside to play for a while longer. He had to get to bed early tonight. Mrs. Stephens was coming over to get him started on some schoolwork tomorrow morning.

While William was outside, Steven called George to ask if they could come over that evening. He and Jane wanted to talk to them about William. George said they would be over soon.

George and Marie arrived 30 minutes later with a cake that George had made. They sat and shared a piece with William and heard all about Patch and his struggles with trying to learn to return a stick. When it was time for William to go to bed, he said goodnight to everyone, but did not give hugs yet. He was still shy about hugging and touching other people.

The four adults went out to the front porch to sit, have coffee and talk.

Steven relayed his conversation with Anna to the others. He told them about asking Stella to listen in to the conversation and that she had taken notes on what was said.

"At this point, I'm inclined to get a lawyer and seek temporary custody of William. I do not believe that he is safe returning to Lewiston. With Anna's work schedule and the fact that she is reluctant to give him any attention at all, I think it would be better for him to stay here with us," explained Steven.

"I think we also need to ask William what he wants to do," said Marie. "After all, Anna is his mother, and I am sure he loves her."

"Marie, I don't think William knows what love is. He is learning because of Patch, but it will take time. Every time he cuddles Patch and Patch licks him, I think he is experiencing the emotion of love. The poor child had never had that feeling before he came here," Jane said.

"What is it you want to do Steven?" asked Marie with a tear running down her cheek.

"I want to hire a lawyer and seek temporary custody of William," stated Steven firmly. "Jane, I haven't talked to you about this, but I firmly believe that William would be in danger if he went back to Lewiston and his mother.

"Let me say something," George said with some force. "Anna is my daughter and I love her and have loved her from the second she was born, but there is some flaw in her character that I cannot understand. She wants all of the attention all of the time. When she walks into a room, she expects all conversation to stop and all eyes to go to her. She has been this way since she was very little."

"Anna resented the birth of her sisters and brother. She said that it was not necessary for us to have more children because we had her. As much as I hate to say it, Steven, I agree with you. William will be much better off staying here in Rawlings where he has family, is physically cared for, and is loved," George stated firmly.

"I agree," added Marie. She had tears running down her face and when she talked, she choked up. After all, this was her precious first-born daughter they were talking about and she wondered what she had done wrong in raising her to cause her to be this way about her own child.

Chapter 4

Steven contacted an attorney he knew who practiced in Colfax, Washington. Thomas Campbell had lived in Colfax for three years. He was a good country lawyer, practicing all kinds of law. He only took on clients that he believed in and that he felt were innocent of the crime or had a good chance of winning the case.

Listening to Steven talk about his wife's nephew and the way he was being raised by his mother, Thomas felt that there was a good chance that Steven and his wife could get at least temporary custody, if not permanent custody.

"I will clear my calendar for next week and come to Rawlings. It will be much easier for me to make a final decision on taking the case or not if I see you, your family and especially William. Does he know about all of this?" asked Thomas.

"No, not yet. We chose not to tell him until we had some guidance from a lawyer," stated Steven.

"Good idea," commented Thomas.

Thomas Campbell arrived in Rawlings by train on Monday September 25th. He was a good looking man, with dark brown hair. He was 32 years old and had practiced law for six years. He went directly to the hotel to check in. Jane happened to be at the desk when he arrived and introduced herself. "I am Jane Taylor. My husband Steven contacted you. His office is right behind the post office, so you will have some privacy to talk. I am on duty here for another two hours and can join you then."

"Thank you, Jane. I would like to go to my room and freshen up a bit before meeting with your husband if you don't mind," Thomas asked.

"Certainly. Your room is at the top of the stairs, to the left. Room 203," explained Jane.

Thomas came downstairs a half hour later and went to Steven's office. He knocked and the door was opened by George. "Hello! My name is George Seevers and this is my wife Marie. Anna Jones is our daughter and William is our only grandchild."

"Thomas, I am Steven Taylor. I felt that George and Marie should be included in this conversation because of their relationship to Anna and William."

All of them sat down and Thomas asked them to give him an idea of what the problem was. George started by giving some background information on Anna; the fact that she was a bully in school, resented the birth of her sisters and brother, was rude to her aunts when they were pregnant and generally resented anyone who received more attention than she did.

Marie continued with telling Thomas about Anna leaving to work on the steamship, meeting and marrying Will Jones on the ship and being left in

Astoria. She told him about Will telling Anna that he would be back for her in three months.

George continued by explaining that he asked their friends the Sorenson's to pick Anna up in Astoria and take her to their home in Portland.

Marie continued with Anna's pregnancy and how she and George were in Portland when William was born. Marie explained, "It was a difficult birth for Anna, mainly because she would not cooperate and do what the doctor or anyone else said. After William was born, she would have nothing to do with him. She named him after his father and that was all. I had to force her to hold him. She would not feed him or change him. George and I brought them back here to Rawlings. I thought she would settle down and take care of her son.

At that time, Jane walked into the room with coffee for everyone. Jake, the evening clerk at the hotel desk arrived early so Jane asked him to take over the desk for her so she could be with her husband and parents.

Steven continued the story of Anna and William moving to Lewiston, Idaho. He told Thomas about Anna's job at a saloon and William being alone in the evenings with no one to take care of him. He explained about his eating habits and about him never going to school.

George continued with Anna and William making what the family thought was a visit to Rawlings to see the family, but turning out to be

About Anna abandoning William here and returning to Lewiston alone.

"Okay! Let me ask you some questions," said Thomas. "That you know of, does Anna ever contact William?"

They all answered "No."

"Does Anna ever send any money to William or to you for his care?"

They all answered "No."

"Do you know if she has contacted him in any way?" asked Thomas.

They all answered "No."

That you know of, has any other person ever contacted him on her behalf?" Thomas continued.

They all answered "No".

Thomas sat there for a minute and then said, "*It sounds* to me like Anna is a narcissist." Everyone in the room nodded. Marie was openly crying. George put his arm around her to try and comfort her. "This is my daughter we are talking about," cried Marie.

Thomas answered soothingly, "I know Mrs. Seevers and I am very sorry for being so blunt, but please know that this is not your fault. Narcissism is a personality disorder. It is not known what causes it, but it can be destructive to those around the narcissist. Mrs. Seevers, again I emphasis that neither you nor George caused this in your daughter. Steven, you explained to me over the phone that you and Jane want to seek temporary custody of William. Is that correct?" asked Thomas.

Steven looked at Jane and she nodded. "Yes, it is. We feel he would be much better off here with us where he has supervision and a loving family to watch over him. These are the notes of the conversation I had with Anna over the phone the day before I called you. I had asked our switchboard operator to listen in on the call and she offered to take notes of the conversation. She was very thorough."

"Okay. It is getting on towards supper time and I am starved. It there a good diner in Rawlings?" Thomas asked.

Everyone in the room laughed. "Yes. This hotel has the best. George owns the hotel and was the head chef for years. He still does most of the baking," explained Jane. "Please join us for supper. I will round up William and we all can have supper here."

"Thank you. I would enjoy that. I am anxious to meet William," said Thomas.

William was very quiet at dinner. He was surprised that they were eating at the hotel, but always enjoyed the food and especially his grandfather's desserts.

William wasn't sure about the guest they had. He must have been a friend of William and Jane's. He asked a lot of questions, and they were mostly directed toward him.

William was very quiet until Mr. Campbell started talking about his dog. Then William's eyes lit up and he said, "I have a dog too. His name is Patch. What is your dog's name?"

"Her name is Lucy. She just had a litter of puppies. There are six of them. Three boys and three girls. They are all brown with some gold-colored patches on them. As they grow bigger, their color will probably change a little. I really hope not. They are very pretty now," said Mr. Campbell. I would love to meet Patch. He sounds like a great dog. How about you and I taking him for a walk?"

"Okay," said William. "Patch is out in the back with Mr. Clausen. He is the blacksmith and Patch stays with him when I am in the hotel having supper. He is not allowed in the dining room. I don't know why. He can be in the kitchen at Steven and Jane's house."

"I think it is probably because other customers in the dining room don't like the idea of a dog being in there," explained Mr. Campbell. "They just don't understand dogs I guess," Mr. Campbell said with a smile on his face.

William and Thomas picked up Patch and started walking away from the center of town and the hotel. Patch ran ahead of them for a time, then turned around to see where William was and came running back for a pet and an ear rub. Thomas gave him an ear rub also and Thomas had a new friend for life. Anyone who gave Patch an ear rub was his friend.

"Your grandpa said you used to live in Lewiston, Idaho with your mother. I have been to Lewiston. It is a nice town. Did you like it there?" asked Thomas.

"It was okay, I guess. I like it here better. I get to do more things here," said William in a quiet voice.

"Lewiston is a much bigger town than Rawlings. It seems that there would be a lot more to do there," mused Thomas.

"My mother did not let me do anything. I had to stay inside while she was at work," explained William.

"Where did your mother work. Maybe I know the place," asked Thomas.

"She worked at the Lucky Lady Saloon," said William.

"Did your sitter play games with you or read to you?" asked Thomas.

"I didn't have a sitter," William said very quietly.

"I'm sorry to hear that. You must have been very lonesome," commented Thomas.

"Yea, but not now. I have a lot to do. I have to take care of Patch and Mrs. Stephens comes every day to teach me to read. She is also teaching me my numbers so I will be able to count. I really like her. She is very nice to me and sometimes makes me laugh," said William with a big grin on his face. "She reads to me and tells me funny stories."

"Don't you miss your mother though?" asked Thomas.

"Sometimes but I don't miss her hitting me. No one hits me here, even if I do something I am not supposed to. Mama called me bad names, and no one here calls me bad names. They think I'm okay," explained William.

"I think you're okay too, William," stated Thomas.

William grinned at Thomas and then asked, "Mr. Campbell, why are you asking me all of these questions?"

"William, your Uncle Steven, and Aunt Jane would like you to live with them all of the time and not have to go back to Lewiston. They have asked me to help them make that possible. I would ask a judge to make it possible for you to stay here. Would you like that?"

"Yes, I would, but my Mama would be very mad. She doesn't like people to do things that she wouldn't agree with. I overheard Uncle Steven talking to grandma and grandpa about Mama being really mad that I had a dog and that she said I didn't deserve one. I sure wouldn't want to go back to Lewiston without Patch. Mama wouldn't let me have him though," William explained.

"If you want to stay here with your aunt and uncle, I will try to make that possible. But only if that is what you want," said Thomas.

"I would like that!" pronounced William.

Thomas Campbell stayed in Rawlings for five days. He talked to Blake and Fiona Stephens about William and also about Anna. They both knew Anna before she married and had William.

Thomas spent several hours with Clyde and Virginia Rodgers, talking about Anna when she was a child in school. Virginia's daughter Josephine was one of the recipients of Anna's bullying while she was in school.

Clyde explained to Thomas how Anna would come into the store every day after school and look at the hair ribbons and the big doll he had on display. Sometimes if another girl would admire the doll,

Anna would make it very clear to her that the doll was hers. Her father would buy it for her.

None of Anna's family wanted to say anything against her as a child, but they were all very upset by her attitude towards William. Jane indicated that William did not know what love was until he was given Patch. He never received any from his mother.

William's Uncle Jeff Jordan said that William had mentioned several times about the men that Anna would bring home after work. They made him sleep on the floor in the closet. He would pretend to be asleep but could hear them. If they caught him awake, they would beat him. All his mother would say was, "Serves you right for being awake when you were supposed to be asleep."

Thomas felt he had a pretty good case for Steven and Jane to receive permanent custody of William instead of temporary custody. The evidence against Anna for child abuse and child abandonment was overwhelming.

Thomas had another conference with George and Marie and Steven and Jane before he went back to Colfax. He told them that he would send an official letter to Anna regarding a hearing on custody. He would talk to the judge and see if the hearing could be held in Rawlings so that the witnesses would not have to travel. Anna would be the one who would have to travel to Rawlings for the hearing.

"What happens if she does not come?" Jane asked.

"She will be in contempt of court and be subject to arrest and confinement," answered Thomas.

"She sure won't like that alternative," stated Steven.

Thomas boarded the train for Colfax on Friday September 29th. On Monday, October 2nd, he talked to Judge Albert Corbin about the Jones case and asked if it was possible to move the case to Rawlings. "There are a lot of potential witnesses Judge, and it would be a massive inconvenience for all of them to have to come here."

"You know Tom, I could use a change of scenery. Let me check my calendar and see if I have some time to go to Rawlings to preside over the hearing," stated Judge Corbin.

"As soon as you let me know the date Judge, I will notify Mrs. Jones. She will have to make arrangements to go to Rawlings from Lewiston," Thomas said.

"By the way Tom, I will issue an order now that Mrs. Jones is to have only supervised contact with her son. She is absolutely not to be alone with him until this matter is settled."

"Yes sir. I will see that the order is read to all concerned," answered Thomas.

Anna enjoyed her job at the bar in the Lewiston Arms Hotel. She had been able to make enough money to move closer to her work and was now living in a much nicer boarding house. She was in a safer neighborhood and was not scared to walk back and forth to work.

On Monday, October 16th Anna received a letter at work from an attorney in Colfax, Washington. She couldn't figure out why she would be getting a letter from an attorney.

She opened the letter, read it, and yelled at no one in particular. Her boss Joe Archer looked at her with anger in his eyes. "What the hell!" he said.

Anna threw the letter at him and said, "Read this!"

He read the letter and was as angry as she was. He was angry because she would miss work if she went to Rawlings, and he had no one to replace her.

Anna went to the phone and called the switchboard in Rawlings and asked for Steven. Stella rang through to Steven, but stayed on the line so that she could take notes. She knew the call was from Anna Jones.

"You cannot have my son. He is my property. I am coming to Rawlings to get him and bring him back here. Because of your stupid actions, he will no longer live in Rawlings. And I am not taking that damn dog. He cannot have a dog here. I will not allow it. You have his things packed and ready for me to get him. I am not staying in that town any longer than I have to," Anna yelled.

"I am sorry Anna, but there is a court injunction against you taking William out of Rawlings or being alone with him. You must have someone with you at all times when you are with him," explained Steven very calmly.

"Don't count on it," Anna screamed and hung up the phone.

Steven went in to the switchboard where Stella gave him the notes that she took. He asked her to phone Susan at the JSJ Ranch.

Stella rang Susan through to Steven. "Susan, I want to bring William out to stay with you for a few days. Anna received the letter from the lawyer and is on her way here to pick him up and take him back to Lewiston, without Patch."

"Bring him out right away. We will keep him busy here for a few days. Patch will enjoy being able to run with the other dogs," said Susan.

"Thanks Susan," said Steven.

Steven headed for home to explain to Jane and William what was happening. He and Jane packed some of William's things along with Patch's food bowl and blanket before they all three climbed into the buggy and headed for the ranch.

Stella informed George and Marie of what was happening. They were so sad that this was happening with their daughter but knew that William had to be protected from her. She could seriously hurt him if she had the opportunity.

"William, we would like to talk to you for a minute," said Steven. "Your mama has told me that she is very angry because we are trying to get legal custody of you, and she is coming to pick you up and take you back to Lewiston with her. As we have told you, the judge said that right now, she cannot be alone with you. There must be another person with you at all times when you are with her."

"Because she is so mad, we are afraid she will hurt you, so we have decided to take you out to the ranch for a while. We did not talk to you before we made the decision and I hope it is okay with you," asked Steven.

"Can Patch come too," begged William.

"Of course, he can. Where you go, Patch goes," answered Steven with a smile on his face. "Aunt Jane and I have already packed some of your things and Patch's bowl and pillow and are ready to go. Aunt Susan has invited us to supper, and you know what a good cook she is. We don't want to keep her waiting."

Anna boarded the train to Rawlings with anger. She had no luggage with her except a small bag with some personal items in it. Her plan was to get William and return to Lewiston on the afternoon train. She could care less about some phony court order. William was her son and he belonged to her. She didn't want him, but she did not want anyone else to have him either.

William was a bother to her. And a dog was out of the question. She would not have that filthy thing in her room.

During the train ride to Rawlings, she was trying to figure out what she would do with him. She didn't have any space in her room for him. Maybe she could put a bed on the floor in the closet for him. He would be out of the way, and she could close the door when she had company.

Food was another problem. How was she going to feed him. The little brat didn't need more than one meal a day. She would do like she did before, only feed him one meal a day. He would have to get by with that. She wasn't going to spend any more money on him than she had to.

When Anna left the train in Rawlings, she stormed across the road to the hotel. The door slammed behind her as she walked in. "Where is he?" she yelled at Jane.

"Hello Anna. It's nice to see you. Your father is in the kitchen if that is who you are asking about," Jane said in a calm voice.

At that moment, Steven stepped out of his office. He had seen Anna walking across the road from the depot and knew what was coming.

"No! Where is that kid of mine. I am ready to take him back to Lewiston and I want him here immediately," demanded Anna.

"As I told you on the phone Anna, there is a court order barring you from removing William from Rawlings and from being alone with him," explained Steven.

"He is my child, and I can take him anywhere I want. No judge can tell me what to do with my own child," screamed Anna.

At that moment, Judge Albert Corbin walked into the lobby of the hotel. He had heard the screaming from the hallway upstairs and decided to make an entrance now instead of waiting for a formal introduction.

"I am afraid you are wrong Mrs. Jones. I am Judge Albert Corbin and I have the legal right to limit your contact with your son. As ordered in the decree issued on October 25, 1905, you are not to remove your son from Rawlings, or the surrounding area and you are not to be alone with him."

While Anna was busy sputtering at what Judge Corbin had told her, Thomas Campbell walked into the lobby from the dining room. He walked up to Anna, put his hand out to shake hers and said, "Hello Mrs. Jones, I am Thomas Campbell. I am the attorney who sent you the letter regarding the custody of your son."

Instead of taking his hand, Anna slapped him hard across the face, whirled around and left the lobby screaming for her mother.

Thomas, Judge Corbin, Steven, and Jane were all in shock at Anna's actions. Jane again wondered what had happened to her to make her so hard and unfeeling towards her son. She had always had problems, but never to this extent.

Marie was doing some sewing for Susan. She was sitting in her parlor enjoying a late fall sun coming through the window, when the door burst open and Anna stormed in.

"Anna, what are you doing here?" asked Marie. "You did not let us know you were coming."

"Where is William?" Anna demanded. "I'm going to take him back to Lewiston with me. He is being spoiled here and I won't have a spoiled child. He needs discipline, not spoiling. Where is he?"

"Anna, William is not here. He is visiting a friend and has been asked to spend the night. The court says that you are not to take him out of Rawlings, nor can you be alone with him," Marie explained. "There is nothing we can do about it. Until the judge says differently that order stands Also, you have to be here for the hearing. If you are not here, you will be in contempt of court and subject to a fine and time in jail," said Marie.

"That Judge is a joke and the lawyer Steven and Jane have is a wimp. I can best them both," Anna boasted.

"Why are you acting this way, Anna? You know that William would be better off here with his family looking after him. If he is with you, he is alone most of the time," Marie pleaded.

Anna ignored her mother and turned around and stormed out of the house. She would talk to her father. She could usually get what she wanted from him.

Anna found George sitting outside the back door of the diner drinking a cup of coffee with Steven and Jane's lawyer.

"Hello Papa," she said to her father. George looked up into his daughter's face and wanted to cry. Her expression had become so hard. She wasn't his little girl anymore.

"Hello Anna. Don't ask me where he is because I will not tell you. If you truly want to see him, I will bring him here and you can visit with him. But you will not try to get me to let you take him back to Lewiston with you," George stated very firmly.

Anna was defeated this time, but she knew there had to be a way to get William and take him back to Lewiston. She would think on it and get back to Lewiston as soon as she could.

When Anna returned to Lewiston and to work at the Lewiston Arms Hotel, her boss Joe Archer was not happy with her for leaving. He was forced to work her shift because he did not have a replacement for her.

When she walked into the saloon, Joe was there working her shift. He looked at her and frowned. "Did you bring your kid with you?" he asked Anna.

"No! I didn't even see him. There was a judge there in the hotel who said that there was some paper filed with the courts that says I cannot take him out of Rawlings and that I cannot even see him unless someone is with us," Anna explained.

"That's probably good Anna. You don't have room for him, nor do you have anyone to take care of him while you are working. He is most likely better off where he is," said Joe.

"But he's mine. No one takes away from me what belongs to me. He is my property, and it is stealing when they take him away," explained Anna.

Joe looked at her with a stunned look on her face. He had never heard someone say their child was their property. "Who would take care of him while you are working?" asked Joe.

"He's perfectly capable of taking care of himself. He's ten years old for heaven's sake," hissed Anna.

"Do you mean you leave him home alone from noon until you get home at night?" Joe asked astounded.

"Sure, he's always been okay," answered Anna with a matter-of-fact attitude.

"I'll say right now that kind of attitude and your behavior aren't going to get you very far with a judge. No one is going to like the idea of you leaving him home alone for such a long time. Do you have supper prepared for him ahead of time?" asked Joe.

"No! He only needs to eat one meal a day. He does just fine with breakfast. He doesn't need any more food," explained Anna.

"Anna, you are in for a big shock. You are not only going to lose custody of your son, but you could be prosecuted for child abuse or child neglect," explained Joe.

"I have said before, I will allow no one to take away from me what belongs to me, and William belongs to me," Anna declared.

Chapter 5

William loved being at the ranch. Uncle Jeff was teaching him how to ride a horse. It was a little scary at first, but he was getting used to the horse and to being so high off of the ground.

Patch didn't like him being on the horse. He sat and whined all the time he was riding. William figured he was afraid of the horse because it was so much bigger than he was.

Aunt Susan worked with him in the mornings, teaching him to read. He didn't know that she used to be a teacher. She was really patient with him when he made mistakes, especially in his numbers.

William knew his mother had been in Rawlings and was glad he didn't have to see her. He was afraid she would take him back to Lewiston and he knew that she would not let Patch go with him. He really wanted to stay in Rawlings. He liked living with Uncle Steven and Aunt Jane. They paid a lot of attention to him and listened to what he had to say. His mama never listened to him.

Uncle Jeff was leading him around the corral on the horse when they heard the dinner bell ring. Uncle

Jeff helped him down from the saddle and William led the horse back to his stall.

He was also learning how to take care of the horse. He would give it a good rub down as far as he could reach. He wasn't tall enough to reach the back, and neck, so he did the sides and legs. Then he made sure there was fresh water and feed for him before he went in to wash up.

When he went inside, he was surprised to see Aunt Jane and Uncle Steven there along with Judge Corbin and Mr. Campbell, the lawyer. They had been invited to dinner also.

"Hello William. It is good to see you again. How is Patch doing? Is he learning to bring the stick back to you?" asked Judge Corbin.

William grinned. "Sometimes, but if he sees something that he wants to run after, he forgets about the stick." Judge Corbin laughed at that. "Sounds like something a puppy would do," replied the Judge.

"Let's sit down to dinner please," Susan asked. "Cora has worked hard on the meal."

"It sure smells good," said Steven and sat down next to Jane.

William sat down next to Jane on the other side. He wondered why the Judge and lawyer were there for dinner too. He was a little scared that they were going to tell him that he had to go back to Lewiston with his mother. He didn't want to leave.

The group of people ate dinner quietly with only a little quiet conversation between them. After they finished eating, they went into the study to sit and talk. Steven asked William to join them for a while. "Invite Patch to join us too William. He can curl up by the fire and have a nap," said Uncle Jeff.

"William, would you mind if we talked a little about when you lived in Lewiston with your mother?" asked Judge Corbin.

"No," mumbled William. "But please don't tell me I have to go back to Lewiston with her. I want to stay here. She won't let me have Patch, and I don't want to leave him here."

"I'm sorry for scaring you, William. I will definitely not make you go back to Lewiston with your mother. I am trying to find a way to keep you here in Rawlings legally. I need to ask you some questions though and some of the questions will not be easy for you to answer. If you are uncomfortable answering, please tell me," Judge Corbin asked.

"Ok," mumbled William.

"William, when you lived with your mother, did you have a baby-sitter while your mother was at work?" asked Judge Corbin.

"Sometimes the lady that lived downstairs would come up to see if I was okay," William said. "She never came into our room. She always hollered from the doorway."

"Did your mother have supper ready for you before she went to work?" asked the judge.

"No. Mama said I didn't need more than one meal a day. She would fix me a large breakfast. I had to eat all of it, and it made me sick. I would throw up in the bushes outside."

"Did your mama know that you threw up?"

"No. I didn't tell her. She would have been very mad because I wasted the food that she spent good money for. You know, I never knew what they called it good money. I don't know the difference between good and bad money," mused William.

"Did your mother hit you, William?" Mr. Campbell asked.

"Yea. I was bad a lot of the time. I got dirty a lot, and she didn't like it. She said she had to wash my clothes too often. Sometimes I didn't have extra clothes to wear," William answered.

William, do you want to go back to Lewiston and live with your mama?" Uncle Jeff asked.

"No sir. She won't let me have Patch," William answered emphatically. "Patch needs me to take care of him."

"He sure does!" stated Uncle Jeff.

Aunt Susan decided to call a halt to the questions for now. It was William's bed time, and he needed a bath before bed.

"You go on up and get your bath and I will be up later to finish the story we started last night," said Susan.

"When do I get to go home to Uncle Steven's house?" asked William.

"I think we can come and get you and Patch tomorrow," said Steven.

"I think there is a good chance that you will get custody of William," Judge Corbin said to Steven and Jane. "From my talks with some of the townspeople who knew Anna when she was younger and lived here and from her statements and actions the other day, it seems to me that she is not capable of taking care of a child. There is no evidence of nurturing at all."

"William's comments tonight pretty much sealed it," said Thomas. "He obviously does not want to live with his mother. He also does not want to be separated from his dog," Thomas added.

"This is not only a custody case, but also a case of child abuse and child neglect. Anna Jones could be subject to jail time if found guilty," commented Thomas.

"Please, let's remember that Anna is George and Marie's daughter, and she is Susan's and my niece," said Jane. "We are having a hard time trying to figure out what went wrong with her, but we still love her."

"I understand and will try to take that into consideration, but the first thing we have to think about is William and his welfare," the judge said.

Jane had tears in her eyes as she said, "Thank you. I am also concerned with William's welfare, but I am also concerned about my mother. She is devastated about Anna."

"I know she is, and I am very sorry, but again, William is our main concern now," Judge Corbin said.

The ranch was like a big playground to William. He could be outside playing with Patch or riding horses or watching the cowboys breaking the horses that Uncle Jeff bought from the Indians. He really liked all of the ranch hands. They were all very nice to him, but he liked being at Uncle Steven's and Aunt Jane's house best. When he was there, he felt like he was home. He had never felt that way before. Every place that he lived with his mama was just a room, not a home. When he was at Steven and Jane's, he had his own bedroom with his own things in it. And Patch could be inside the house and even sleep on his bed with him.

William was learning about love and what it meant to love someone or something. He had never experienced that feeling before.

He knew he loved Patch, and he knew Patch loved him back. He also was pretty sure that he loved Steven and Jane and they loved him back. In fact, he was pretty sure that all of his aunts and uncles loved him. He was still not sure he loved them back. He knew he liked them a lot, but love was something different. He wasn't sure what that was. He didn't know how to relate love, other than the feeling he had for Patch and the feeling that Patch seemed to have for him.

On Saturday, Steven and Jane went out to the ranch to get William and take him home. They had a quick lunch and then headed back to Rawlings. They were well into the month of October, and they were watching the weather turn cold early this year. Steven thought they were going to be in for a cold and snowy winter. They probably would not venture too far away from Rawlings during the late fall and winter months.

Thomas Campbell, Steven, and Jane's lawyer indicated that the hearing for custody of William would be held as soon as possible because of the weather. Anna would be compelled to be there for the hearing. The weather very rarely slowed the train traffic, so it was possible for her to be there on fairly short notice.

Steven and Jane were nervous about the hearing but were anticipating a positive outcome.

Fiona Stephens was helping William with his school work. William's aunt Irene was the town's school teacher, but she did not have the time to spend with William on an individual basis. Fiona had been the teacher before Irene so was fully qualified to teach William.

Fiona was surprised at the speed in which William was learning. He was a smart young man. It was terrible that he did not get the education he needed before he was ten years old.

Fiona was sure it would not take him long to be up to his grade level or beyond. She had weekly meetings with Irene to assess his progress and to decide when he would move into the classroom instead of being tutored at home.

"Irene, I think William is about ready to go into the classroom for instruction. He is reading at the fifth-grade level now and has math skills at a ninth-grade level. He is a very intelligent young man. He could be so much further along if he would have been in school from the beginning," Fiona explained.

"I know, but my niece didn't see fit to follow up on his schooling. We don't know what happened or why she takes no interest in William at all. The whole family loves him. He is learning about living in a big family and having some privileges given to him. He has never had that," related Irene.

"Judge Corbin talked to me about William. I do hope he will be able to stay here in Rawlings. It doesn't sound like his home life is very good," said Fiona.

"We hope he can too. Thanks for the information about his being in a classroom. I will talk to Steven and Jane and see when they want to start him in the classroom. It might be after the custody hearing. It would be a shame if he went back to Lewiston with his mother, but that is always a possibility," explained Irene.

Thomas Campbell was in Rawlings again to talk to them about the hearing. Judge Corbin had set the date of the hearing for Tuesday, November 28th. Both Thomas and Judge Corbin would come to Rawlings for the hearing. They want to be sure that Anna would be there, and she would be more apt to come to Rawlings than to Colfax.

There were a few more people Thomas wanted to talk to and one of them was Irene Seevers, the schoolteacher. She was not only William's school teacher, but she was also his aunt.

Thomas knocked on the door of Irene' house after school one day, hoping to talk to her about William. "Hello," Irene said cautiously when she answered the door.

"Hello, Miss Seevers. I am Thomas Campbell, Steven, and Jane's lawyer for their case for custody of William Jones. May I speak with you for a moment?" asked Thomas.

"Certainly. Please come in. I was about to fix my supper. Would you like to join me?" asked Irene.

"That would be very nice, but I didn't come to beg a meal from you," Thomas said with a smile on his face.

"I have plenty for both of us. It happens to be leftover chicken soup that my brother-in-law George made. He also baked an extra loaf of bread for me. I really cannot resist his homemade bread," said Irene.

Thomas nodded and said, "I have tasted his bread and I agree with you. It is very hard to resist."

They sat down to eat their supper in Irene's cheerful kitchen. "I wanted to talk to you about William. The hearing for the custody case is going to be on the 28th of November and I want to get as much of my research done as possible so that I can present a complete case to the judge," Thomas explained.

"What do you want to know from me?" asked Irene.

"I want to know about William's schooling. What was his grade level when he first started school here?" asked Thomas.

"When he first came here, he came to school for only one day. It was obvious that he had had no schooling at all in Lewiston. Apparently, Anna sent him off to school, but William never got there. According to William, she would feed him a huge breakfast and make him eat all of it even if he was full. She would send him off to school and he would go into the bushes not far from their rooming house and throw up most of his breakfast. He told me that he didn't really feel good after that and did not go on to school. After his first day in class here, he ran out of the room and ran the opposite way from Steven and Jane's house. Steven found him and brought him home. He said that he was going back to Lewiston where at least his mother did not keep track of him all day," explained Irene.

"Steven, Jane, and Fiona Stephens talked about his situation and decided it would be best to keep him at home until he at least learned to read a little bit. Fiona has been tutoring him at home and he has done remarkably well. If he had been in school since the first grade, he would have been so far ahead by now. I talked to Fiona yesterday and we decided that it is time for William to start going to classes. He is reading at grade level now and needs the socialization with the other students," Irene commented.

Irene and Thomas finished their supper and had moved into the sitting room. Irene excused herself to go back into the kitchen and pour them a cup of coffee. When she returned to the sitting room, she found Thomas looking at all of the books she had on shelves around the room. "I am impressed with your book collection. It looks like some of these books are old," mentioned Thomas.

"They are old. I don't think I have ever discarded a book. I keep them all. I have been an avid reader since I first started school. My family used to complain because I always had my face in a book. My brother-in-law George is a reader also. He was raised in an orphanage and was taught to read by one of the matrons. She instilled in him a life-long love of reading. In fact, when he was young, he read a story about Lewis and Clark and the Pacific Ocean. He had a lifelong desire to see the Ocean and it wasn't until William was born that he and my sister were able to visit the Lewis and Clark encampment and Cannon Beach on the Oregon Coast. They both love it there and have expressed a desire to retire there sometime," Irene explained.

"I was able to see the Pacific Ocean at Long Beach, Washington two years ago. It is a beautiful beach, and the waters of the Pacific Ocean are truly incredible," said Thomas. I must get back to the hotel and write up some notes for the hearing. Thank you so much for the supper. It was delicious. And thank you for the information about William. The more information we have the better Steven and Jane's chances of getting custody of him are. And thank you for letting me see your library. Your books are impressive," said Thomas.

"You are most welcome. All we want is what is best for William. We love Anna but feel that she has pretty much sealed her fate by her attitude and actions," said Irene.

Thomas Campbell felt that there was a good cause for charging Anna Jones with child neglect and child abuse. From all of the comments he had listened to, it was evident that Anna did not have any regard for her son's welfare at all. She only considered him a possession of hers to do with as she pleased.

He was going to make a proposal to Judge Corbin that, if Anna Jones would voluntarily give up custody of her son William Jones to Steven and Jane Taylor, then charges would not be brought against her for child neglect and child abuse. If she accepted this proposal they would not have to go through the ordeal of a custody hearing and she would not be subject to any prison time.

Thomas went back to Colfax to give his proposal to Judge Corbin before he left for Rawlings and the custody hearing. When he went into the judge's chambers, he saw that Judge Corbin was knee deep in paperwork.

The judge stood up and greeted Thomas with handshake. "Hello Thomas. What can I do for you today?" asked Judge Corbin.

"This is in regard to the William Jones custody hearing. I have a proposal to give to you for your consideration," said Thomas.

He presented the written proposal to Judge Corbin. The judge read the proposal and looked at Thomas. "This might work. I can present this proposal to Anna Jones and see what her reaction is. I will give her 10 days to respond. If she does not respond to my letter, we will have to proceed with the hearing. If she does not show up for the hearing, she will be in contempt of court and be subject to arrest and confinement," said Judge Corbin.

A letter was drafted to Anna Jones regarding the proposal to relinquish custody of William Henry Jones to Steven and Jane Taylor of Rawlings, Washington.

The letter read, "Dear Miss Jones: In the matter of the minor child, William Jones Jr., you are requested to surrender custody of said child to Steven and Jane Taylor of Rawlings, Washington. Your actions towards William Jones Jr. require me to ask you to relinquish custody. If you do not relinquish custody, William Jones Jr. will become a ward of the State of Washington and you will be sent to jail for Child Abuse and Child Neglect. You have ten days to respond to this letter. If you do not respond, you will be arrested and William Jones Jr. will go into an orphanage in the State of Washington until he can be placed into a home."

When Anna received the letter from Judge Corbin, she went ballistic. The only address the courts had for her was the Lewiston Arms Hotel saloon. She was at work when she received the letter and her boss, Joe Archer had to calm her down and find out what was going on.

Anna handed the letter to Joe to read. "Anna, you need to get a lawyer of your own. They are going to shaft you if you don't have someone on your side," Joe said.

"I can't afford a lawyer. I am barely making ends meet now," cried Anna. "I can't believe that my family is doing this to me. They think I am cruel to the kid, they are the ones who are being cruel to me," Anna said in disgust.

"You take the rest of the evening off and go home and think about your options. Unfortunately, if anyone asked me, I would have to admit that you have not taken very good care of your son. Think about what it would mean to you not to have to worry about him. Let someone else pay for his upkeep. Hasn't it been a relief to not have to spend money on him these past few months?" asked Joe.

"Yea, I guess so. But it is the principle of the thing. I don't like to have someone take my possessions away from me," Anna admitted.

Anna went back to her room at the boarding house. She had a small kitchen in her room and was able to fix some simple meals for herself. Most of the time, she was at work during supper time and did not eat with the other boarders. She fixed herself a bowl of soup and sat and thought about her situation with William. She really didn't want the responsibility of having him around. He would interfere with her social life and cause nothing but problems.

The thought of going to jail for child abuse or neglect was terrifying to her. She could not let that happen. She supposed that she was not very nice to her son, but what else was she to do with him?

After a lot of thought, Anna wrote a letter to Thomas Campbell saying that she would relinquish custody of William to Steven and Jane Taylor, her aunt and uncle. She signed the letter and then at the bottom of the page, she wrote in large letters, "GOOD RIDDANCE".

After writing the letter, she put her coat on and went out to post it. She wanted the distasteful business to be over with.

Chapter 6

Clyde and Virginia Rodgers were blissfully happy with their life together. Clyde had taken to married life better than anyone thought he would. He loved and admired Virginia's six children and got along well with all of them.

None of the Kingman children missed their father. He was in prison in Walla Walla, and they all hoped that he would stay there. He was in prison for the death of his newborn son in October 1887. His sentence was extended because he had a fight in prison that caused the death of another inmate.

In October 1905, Virginia unexpectedly received a letter from Otis. He had never accepted the fact that they were divorced and that she had remarried. He told her in the letter that he expected all of the boys to be at home and working the farm. He would be back to take over the running of the family.

"Honey, I think you need to contact that lawyer Steven and Jane used for William's custody case. If Otis does receive parole and comes back to find you are married and the farm was sold, he could cause a lot of trouble." Clyde explained to Virginia.

Thomas Campbell happened to be in Rawlings visiting Irene Seevers. Virginia saw him in the hotel lobby one afternoon and asked to speak to him in private.

"What can I do for you Virginia?" asked Thomas.

"I received this letter from my ex-husband. He is in prison in Walla Walla and is up for parole in another month. He has been in prison since 1887 and has never accepted the fact that we are divorced. I sold the farm after he was gone and moved into a small house in town."

"What did he go to prison for?" asked Thomas.

"Manslaughter, child and spousal abuse," stated Virginia matter-of-factly. "By withholding food from me, he caused our baby to die of malnutrition and he did not take care of my needs after the baby was born. I almost bled to death."

"Do you feel this letter is a threat to you and your children?" asked Thomas.

"I certainly do," Virginia said emphatically.

Thomas notified the parole board at the state prison in Walla Walla of Otis Kingman's letter and informed them that Virginia Kingman Rodgers considered the letter a threat to both her and to her children.

Thomas received a letter back from the parole board indicating that they would take his letter under consideration in their deliberations regarding Otis Kingman's parole bid.

Thomas Campbell was spending a lot of time in Rawlings. He was seeing Irene Seevers on a fairly regular basis. "My dear, would you like to have dinner with me on Friday evening,?" Thomas asked Irene. "The hotel dining room does a fine pot roast."

"I would love to have dinner with you Thomas," answered Irene.

Irene got a little nervous when Thomas asked her out. She had never had a suitor before, and she was not sure how to act. She did love the feeling she got when she was with him. She thought maybe she was falling in love with him.

December 1905 was a cold and snowy month. Christmas decorations were going up all over town and the hotel was beautifully decorated. George had found a tall evergreen tree for the lobby and asked the school children to make decorations for it.

Irene had brought the whole class to the hotel on Wednesday the 13th of December to put their decorations on the tree.

"That is the prettiest tree I have very seen," declared George. All of the children were so proud of their contributions to the tree.

Because of the weather, Thomas decided to stay in Rawlings instead of going back to Colfax. He had no pressing business there until after the first of the year and he wanted to be with Irene and her family on Christmas.

Thomas did not have a family nearby. His mother and stepfather lived in Baltimore, and he hadn't seen them in years. He went to Harvard Law School, but decided to move West when his mother married his stepfather. Unfortunately, Thomas did not get along very well with him and in order to avoid conflict with his mother, he moved West.

He went to Seattle first, but the city was too big and rowdy for his satisfaction. He wanted a smaller, more rural area where he could practice all kinds of law.

Thomas saw an advertisement in the paper about the town of Colfax, Washington needing an attorney. He answered the ad, interviewed, and got the job. But he was very lonesome in Colfax. He knew very few people and seemed to have more clients out of town than in town.

Thomas picked Irene up at her house and they walked to the hotel dining room. It was warm and cozy with the feeling of Christmas all around them.

Thomas and Irene were seated at a table in the center of the dining room. "Will you excuse me for just a moment Irene, I have a quick question to ask George. I will be right back."

"All right," answered Irene with a puzzled look on her face.

Thomas went back to the kitchen area to find George.

"I need to ask you a question George," said Thomas

"What is it? As you can see Thomas, I don't have much time right now," George told him.

"I need to ask you if it is okay for me to ask Irene to marry me. I didn't know who else to ask," said Thomas.

George looked at Thomas and got a big grin on his face. "Are you going to take her back to Colfax?"

"No! I am going to move my practice to Rawlings." I really do love that lady and want her to be my wife," reassured Thomas.

"Okay by me!" George said as he got back to his baking.

"I'm sorry I had to leave you. I had a question I had to ask George. I am back now and I'm all yours for the rest of the evening.," Thomas explained to Irene.

The two enjoyed a venison steak dinner with steamed vegetables and freshly baked bread. George had baked a mincemeat pie and they had that with rum sauce on it for desert. Both of them were stuffed when they left the table to walk back to Irene's place.

They were half way to her house when Thomas stopped her, turned her around to face him and kissed her. "I am so in love with you Irene and want to ask if you will marry me," Thomas asked.

Irene was stunned at the proposal. She had not expected it. She knew that she was in love with Thomas but had no idea how he felt.

"I am stunned Thomas. I had no idea that you felt that way about me. I have known for some time that I was falling in love with you. And yes, I will marry you, but I'm not sure that I want to move back to Colfax,"

"That is not a problem. I am moving my practice here to Rawlings. There is more work for me in this town and it seems the farmers and ranchers around here are always needing a lawyer to help resolve land and water issues," explained Thomas.

"I would like to petition the school board to let me continue to teach school after we are married. Normally, married women are not allowed to continue to teach," Irene said.

Thomas and Irene reached her house. It was getting colder outside, and Thomas decided that he had better go back to his room in the hotel. Otherwise, he would not want to go.

Virginia Rodgers received another letter from Otis demanding that she and the boys be available at the farm when he was granted parole and came home.

Virginia was truly scared that Otis would somehow be released and come back to Rawlings. She took the letter to Thomas Campbell. "Thomas, I have received another letter from my ex-husband and am scared that he will be granted parole and come back here. He will not accept the fact that I divorced him and am remarried. I am truly afraid for Clyde also.

"I will write Otis a letter explaining the situation and send him a copy of the divorce decree and the sale papers on the farm. That should convince him that you are no longer his wife," Thomas explained to Virginia.

Thomas sent a letter to Otis explaining the situation along with a copy to the parole board. With the threats he has issued to Virginia, he should not be eligible for parole at this time.

To be certain that Otis did not receive parole, Thomas decided to go to the parole hearing in Walla Walla. An outside, interested party was allowed to testify at the hearing. Thomas would testify on behalf of Virginia and Clyde Rodgers and the Kingman children.

Irene was worried about Thomas going to Walla Walla, but he assured her that he would be fine. It was a protected hearing with guards there to protect the parole board members and anyone else that might be present.

Thomas boarded the commuter train at noon and after a stop in Dayton, would arrive in Walla Walla at 4:00 PM. The hearing was at 10:00 the next morning.

Thomas had never been to a parole hearing before and found the process somewhat daunting. He was ushered into a waiting room and told that he would be called when it was time for Otis' hearing.

Two hours later, Thomas was ushered into a room with a panel of men sitting in front and Otis Kingman at a table facing them. There was a table and chair to the side of the room where Thomas was directed to sit.

The hearing started with a list of the crimes that put Otis in prison in the first place. They then proceeded with a list of his infractions that occurred since he was in prison. After that, Otis was given a chance to speak on his own behalf.

"Sirs, I am needed at home to run my farm. My wife and children are incapable of handling the workload by themselves. My sons have been shipped out to live with strangers. They need supervision and I am the only one who can do that. I am their father."

Thomas was asked if he wanted to speak at that time. "Yes sirs. I am Thomas Campbell, the attorney for Virginia Kingman Rodgers. When Otis Kingman was sentenced to prison for manslaughter, spousal abuse and child abuse, Mrs. Rodgers obtained a divorce from Mr. Kingman. I have a copy of the decree for your files. Mrs. Kingman was awarded full custody of the six living children and full ownership of the Kingman farm. Shortly after being awarded sole ownership of the farm, Mrs. Rodgers sold the farm and moved into town. Her boys had never been allowed to go to school, so could not read or write. They were sent to live and work on the JSJ Ranch in Rawlings. Mrs. Jordan, the wife of the ranch owner, is a former schoolteacher and she worked with the boys for several years and taught them to read, write and count. The oldest boy Seth is now 25 years old and is a valued employee on the JSJ Ranch, as is Daniel, the second son. Bill is 21 years old, is engaged to be married in the Spring and has just purchased a farm just outside of Rawlings."

Thomas continued, "Josephine, their oldest daughter is in nursing school here in Walla Walla. She is 18 years old. James, the fourth son works with his stepfather in the General store and will eventually take it over. And Margaret their youngest daughter is still in school and works on a part-time basis in housekeeping at the hotel in town."

"I also have copies of letters that Mrs. Rodgers received from Mr. Kingman. She sees these letters as a threat to both her and her husband and also to her children. Until Mr. Kingman can accept the fact that Virginia Rodgers is no longer his wife, and his children are grown and have lives of their own, Mr. and Mrs. Rodgers, Mr. Kingman's children, and I as the Rodgers' attorney, do not feel that parole should be granted at this time. Thank you for allowing me to speak at this hearing on behalf of the Rodgers-Kingman family."

When Otis was led out of the hearing room, he looked at Thomas and said angrily to him, "You have not heard the last of this." Otis was put back into handcuffs and leg irons the minute he was out of the hearing room.

The parole board reconvened an hour later with a decision to not grant parole to Otis Kingman at this time.

Otis was angrier than he had ever been when he heard the decision of the board. He trashed his cell and yelled and screamed until the guards put him into solitary confinement to settle down.

Chapter 7

"Are you excited about Christmas this year William?" asked Steven.

"I guess so. I don't know much about Christmas. Mama and I never celebrated. She was always working," William answered.

"Christmas is the time we celebrate the birth of Jesus Christ. We go to church, we sing Christmas Carols and we gather as a family to honor the birth of the Christ Child," explained Steven.

"You had presents in your stocking, didn't you?" asked Jane.

"Why would Mama put presents in my stockings? I had them on my feet," stated William.

Steven and Jane looked at each other and realized that William had never had a Christmas celebration and probably never had a present.

They went on talking about the different things that happened during the holiday season. William was enthralled by the Christmas tree in the lobby of the hotel and wanted to know why they had one there.

"William, we will go tomorrow and cut down a tree to put in our house. Jane and I have some decorations, but maybe you could make some like the kids did at school for the hotel tree," Steven said.

"I know about the tree in the hotel lobby but does everyone have a tree in their house?" asked William.

"A lot of people have trees, but some people don't believe in Christmas, or they just don't want to go to the bother. I have seen some people who have a tree in their yard and they do not want to cut it down, so they leave it there and decorate it outside," answered Steven.

They were all going out to the ranch on Saturday if the weather would let them. George, Marie and Freddie, Bill and Valerie, Thomas and Irene and Steven, Jane and William would all be there. Jeffrey Jr. was going to be home from college for the Christmas holiday and wanted to see everyone.

On Saturday morning everyone met at the front porch of the hotel with their wagons and drove out to the JSJ Ranch together. They were all singing Christmas carols and they could be heard for miles around. There were four wagons traveling all in a row.

When they arrived at the main house, the women went to the kitchen to work on the meal and the men settled in the office to talk about whatever came to mind. The office was the only place in the house that the men could smoke, so they stayed in there.

William and Patch went out in search of Earl, the foreman. William was hoping to have a ride on one of the horses, but it would depend on whether Earl had time to lead him around. Even if he couldn't ride, he liked being around Earl. Earl talked to him and explained things to him like Steven did.

William found Earl just going into the bunkhouse to talk to some of the men. "Hey Sport, how are you doing?" Earl asked William. "I'm fine. How are the horses today?" William asked with hope that Earl would let him ride.

"They are fine, but it is a little cold out for you to ride. The wind is coming up and you would get too cold. You and Patch come into the bunkhouse and sit by the fire with the other men. The other dogs are in there too," Earl stated.

It made William feel very good to know that the men would let him and Patch sit in the bunkhouse with them. He sat and watched some of the hands play a game of poker. Someday when he learned the game better, he would be able to play with them.

Jeff had called down to the bunkhouse and asked that William come back to the main house. Dinner was about to be served and he needed to wash up.

William carried Patch inside his coat while he walked back to the main house. It was getting really cold outside.

All of the ladies had done a superb job fixing the dinner. Everyone ate way too much.

"Hey family! Could I have your attention for a few minutes?" George asked. Everyone quieted down so they could listen to what George had to say. "Marie and I have been talking for a long time about turning the operation of the hotel over to Freddie. We are going to move to Cannon Beach, Oregon. We will not move until the Spring sometime. Our good friends Isaac and Julia Sorenson have been scouting out a house for us to buy and have found the perfect place. It is right on the beach with an ocean view and a view of Haystack Rock."

"Freddie will be 25 years old by the time we leave and he is well ready to take over the running of the hotel. I trust him completely to take care of the hotel and the employees. Steven, I would ask that you continue to keep the books for both the hotel and the restaurant and continue to do the ordering for both."

"With Thomas moving his office to Rawlings, we now have an attorney in town who can take care of any legal problems that may arise."

"I hope that this does not come as too much of a shock for you, but it is time that Marie and I have some alone time. We have spent our whole married life taking care of our family and we are tired. We want this time together while we are still in good health and the beach has always been our dream."

"We also did not want to make any move until William was taken care of," Marie added. "William, we are so happy that you will be making your home with Uncle Steven and Aunt Jane. You are such an important part of our lives, being our grandson. All we have ever wanted for you is that you are happy."

There was a moment of silence after George and Marie made their announcement, but then, everyone started talking at once. The family expressed sorrow that they would be leaving, but joy for them that they will be fulfilling a lifelong dream.

The weather looked like it was going to get worse, so everyone packed up and headed for home. The wind was blowing and it was a cold ride back to Rawlings, but all arrived home safely.

The next day, the main topic of conversation was George and Marie and their pending move to Oregon. Everyone was happy for them, but they would be missed.

Steven Taylor and William Jones bundled up in their warmest coats, hats and boots and headed out looking for the perfect Christmas tree for their house.

Steven knew of a place not far away where there were some perfect trees just the right size.

"We have to be careful that we pick just the right tree. First, it has to fit into the parlor. That is the most important thing, but we need to make sure that there are plenty of trees left to grow for next year. It takes many years for a tree to grow and we do not want to cut down so many that there will be none left," Steven explained.

After leaving the wagon, Steven and William walked into the grove of trees, looking at several trees to judge if they would fit into the parlor. William found one, but it was too tall, then he found one that was too small. They trudged around looking at all the trees. Finally, William found a tree that Steven said was just the right size.

Steven gave William the saw and said "Okay, you can cut this tree." William looked at him with a startled look on his face. "I don't know how to cut down a tree. I have never used a saw before."

"Okay, I will show you how," answered Steven. He put the saw in William's hand, kneeled down on the ground and put the blade to the tree. Then he guided Williams hands in a back-and-forth movement with just enough pressure on the saw to cut into the tree.

"You need to put enough pressure on the saw so that it will continue to cut through the trunk of the tree," explained Steven. He got up and William continued to cut through the trunk.

When the tree started to tip, Steven encouraged William to keep sawing. Finally, the tree fell to the ground and William smiled and shouted, "I did it!"

"You sure did," Steven said as he put an arm around William's shoulder and gave him a squeeze.

William was startled by the gesture but found it very nice. He turned and gave Steven a big bear hug. "Thanks," he said to Steven. "That was fun."

Steven took the trunk end and William the top of the tree and they hauled it back to the wagon and went home.

Steven had a smile on his face and William could not stop talking about cutting down the tree. He ran into the house to tell Aunt Jane all about cutting down the tree.

"Uncle Steven gave me a hug too. I don't remember ever having a hug before," commented William. Jane wanted to cry at that statement, put her arms around William and hugged him tight. "You will have a lot of hugs around here. They mean that we love you and are very glad you live here with us. Now, let's get that tree ready to bring into the house," added Jane as she wiped the tears from her cheeks.

The whole family met for Christmas Eve church services on Sunday, the 24th of December 1905. William had never been to Christmas Eve church before. He loved the music and the play that the children put on. There were angels, three wise men, shepherds, Joseph, Mary, and a doll they used as the baby Jesus. William thought it was a neat story but couldn't figure out why the baby was born in a stable. The only stables he knew about were in back of the hotel and at the ranch. He couldn't imagine anyone having a baby in either one of them.

Christmas morning was full of wonder for William. He woke up, went down to look at the tree and found presents underneath that had his name on them. There were presents from Steven and Jane, from Grandma and Grandpa Seevers, from Bill and Valerie and from Aunt Irene and Mr. Campbell. And he had small presents in a stocking that he had hung by the fireplace. It was a little overwhelming.

William had never been given a present that was wrapped in pretty paper before. On the rare occasions that he got something from his mother, it was given with an explanation of all the money she was spending on him.

Patch even had a present. He was given a big elk bone to chew on and he was content to lay by the fire chewing on his bone most of the day.

The family gathered at the hotel restaurant for a noon dinner on Christmas day. When Uncle Jeff and Aunt Susan arrived, Jeff asked William to come out to the front porch with him. Everyone followed them and there tied up to the rail was the most beautiful horse William had ever seen. Jeff explained that he had just purchased her from the Palouse Indians especially as a gift for William.

William was so startled and surprised that anyone would give him a horse. He was openly crying. Most of the family had never seen him cry. He ran to Jeff and threw himself into his arms. He couldn't say thank you enough times. Then he ran to Aunt Susan and did the same thing.

Jeff explained that the horse would live at the ranch for a while until William was more familiar with riding her and then he could board her at the livery stable if he wanted to or he could leave her at the ranch.

William and Jeff walked the horse back to the stable until dinner was over, then Jeff would take it back to the ranch.

William knew he could visit his horse anytime he wanted to.

On Christmas Eve after church services, Thomas walked Irene home. He knelt down on one knee on her front porch and presented her with a beautiful solitaire diamond engagement ring. Irene was in tears when he put it on her finger.

They went inside to warm up and sit and talk about wedding dates and arrangements.

"Since my parents are leaving in the spring, I would like to be married before they leave," Irene said.

"Do you want a large church wedding," asked Thomas.

"Not really," answered Irene. I have waited awhile to get married and don't feel a large wedding is necessary. What about you? Would you like a large wedding?

"No. I do not have any family close. My parents are in Baltimore and my brother is in New York and he would not come anyway. If it would be okay with you, I would like to have Judge Corbin marry us though. He has been a good friend to me and supported me when I first went into practice in Colfax. He also was very supportive of Steven and Jane's custody case," Thomas stated.

"If we get married in March, we could possibly have the wedding at the ranch. I could check with Susan if that is okay with you?"

"That is perfect with me," said Thomas.

"Now, I had better leave so you can get some sleep. Tomorrow is a big day for all of us," said Thomas as he put his arms around Irene and gave her a big hug and kiss goodnight.

Bill and Valerie were having about the same discussion about wedding dates as Thomas and Irene had. Because her parents were leaving, Valerie wanted to move her wedding date up to March or April before her parents left.

The difference with Bill and Valerie is that they wanted to be married in the church and Valerie wanted her Papa to walk her down the aisle.

George and Marie had talked to their friends the Sorenson's and indicated that they probably would not be able to get to Portland until the latter part of April or early May. Julia Sorenson indicated that that would give them time to have the place reroofed and painted inside before they got there. Julia already knew the colors that Marie had chosen for the different rooms.

Bill and Valerie decided that they would get married on Saturday, April 21, 1906.

Thomas and Irene were going to wait until the summer before they took a honeymoon. Irene was hoping that the school board would at least let her finish the school year as the teacher in Rawlings. She would petition to the school board as soon as possible for a special dispensation.

William was fascinated by all of the wedding talk. He was talking to Jane about it one day and asked, "was my Mama ever married?"

"Yes. She was married to your father. They were married by the captain on the steamboat that they both worked on. Right after they were married, your father signed on as a crew member on a cargo ship headed for China. Your mama was in Astoria, Oregon at the time. Unfortunately, your father's ship went down in a storm in the South China Sea," Jane explained.

"She must not have had a wedding like Valerie and Irene are talking about," William said.

"No, she probably didn't," Jane said.

Steven and Jane were amazed at the questions that William asked. He was curious about everything and was opening up and asking more questions.

He would wander around town and ask questions of Ray at the blacksmith shop and ask questions of Stella, the switchboard operator and ask questions of Jim Barnes, the cook at the hotel restaurant.

Everyone seemed to be aware of William's background and were more than happy to talk to him. Everyone was just happy that he was opening up and becoming comfortable talking to people.

People very rarely talked about or asked about Anna. No one heard from her at Christmas, including William. He didn't seem to miss her at all. Christmas was not something that was celebrated when he was with her anyway, so he did not miss the contact.

William started going back to school in January and loved it. He was accepted by the other students and seemed to be well liked. He was able to keep up very nicely with the classwork and felt comfortable with his classmates.

Irene was thrilled with his progress and so were Fiona and Susan. They all had a vested interest in his progress because they all had a part in tutoring him.

The weather had turned very cold, but there was not a significant amount of snow, so people could get around fairly well in their wagons. The town of Rawlings was still growing. George and Marie noticed that since they moved there in June of 1884, a general store, doctor's clinic, jail, bank, and a church had been built. The school had been added onto and a house built for the school teacher. Several small farms have been built up and three large cattle ranches have been created, including the JSJ Ranch. It was by far the largest in the area. Jeff Jordan kept buying land and built his ranch into a very profitable business.

The gristmill was in operation for several years but was not profitable for the town or the wheat ranchers, so was disbanded about five years after it started. The building was still standing but abandoned. The mill was on the JSJ Ranch property and Jeff was not sure what he was going to do with it as yet.

Jesse Chamberlain was the grist mill operator. When the mill closed, he worked for a while for Jeff Jordan, but finally decided to move on.

Steven received a new Sears Roebuck catalog in the mail. Most of his ordering now was done through the catalog. He could order almost everything that was needed for the general store and for the hotel from the one catalog.

Steven was hoping that he could give up the job of doing all of the ordering. It was taking up more time than he had to give. He was going to teach Bill Kingman how to order supplies for the general store and Freddie was ready to take over the ordering for the hotel and restaurant.

Jim Barnes, the cook at the restaurant was very good at managing the supplies needed and notified Freddie in a timely manner when he needed anything. The food supplies were ordered directly from the vendors and shipped in via train, usually from Portland. The rest of what was needed was ordered from the Sears catalog.

He and William were looking over the catalog in order to buy William some new clothes. He was growing so fast that all of his pants were too short and his shoes were a size too small.

William had been in Rawlings for a little over four months now and it was hard to believe that he had not always been there. He was an important part of the community.

It was also hard to believe that it had been that long since he had seen or had any contact with his mother. Sometimes he thought about her and wondered about her. It was hard to believe that she had never loved him or even cared for him.

He was beginning to know what love was. He loved Patch and his horse and he loved Uncle Steven and Aunt Jane. And he loved his other relatives, but he could not say he loved his mother, not with that same wonderful feeling he had for the others.

Sometimes William felt sad about his mother. He wished he had a mother like the other kids did. Aunt Jane was great and she took good care of him and loved him, but she wasn't his mother.

The town was buzzing about the two weddings coming up this spring. Everyone was very excited for both of the couples.

Even though Thomas and Irene would be married at the ranch and have a small family wedding, the townspeople were happy and excited for them.

Bill and Valerie's wedding would be a bigger affair. They would be married in the Rawlings Christian Church by the Rev. John Simons.

George and Marie were busy making plans for their move to Oregon. They didn't know what to do with their house until Irene mentioned that she and Thomas were going to look for a house with room for an office for Thomas.

"I have the perfect solution," exclaimed George. "You could buy our house. We have an extra room on the main floor that could be used as an office. It would not be hard to even add on and make a separate entrance and an area for a receptionist."

Irene looked at her papa with amazement. She was not sure what Thomas would say, but she liked the idea, but was surprised that her parents would sell their house.

Irene felt like she was in denial that they would leave Rawlings. Their life had been centered around the town and the hotel for so many years and their family had grown up there. It would be very hard for her to see them leave.

"Papa, what if you decide you want to come back," asked Irene.

"We might come back for visits, but not to live. I want to have the complete experience of living at the ocean. Isaac and Julia have found us a lovely little house and we will be very content and comfortable there. I will read, your mama will sew and we will both walk on the beach. We will make new friends and have a marvelous retirement," George explained.

"If we come back for visits, there is always the hotel to stay in. I think Freddie might make us a good deal on the room rate," George said with mischief in his voice.

Irene would be very sad to see them go, but she was embarking on a new adventure with Thomas and her life would change. She would miss getting advice from both her parents though. At least she still had Aunt Susan and Aunt Jane around.

Irene was anxious to talk to Thomas about purchasing her parents' house, but he was visiting a client at one of the outlying farms today and would not be back until tomorrow morning. She was thinking about the possibility of buying her parents' house and remodeling to make a separate entrance.

She and Thomas had not talked about whether they would have children or not. She was 27 years old and felt she was a little old to start her family now, but maybe it would happen. The house would be just perfect to raise a family in.

Bill Kingman and Valerie Seevers were talking about the farm they were buying. The bank had approved the mortgage. Bill had been very good about saving his salary from the JSJ Ranch and had a substantial down payment. With Jeff and Susan Jordan's recommendation, they were given the loan.

"The barn and outbuildings are in pretty good shape, but the house needs some work. The porch needs to be repaired and it needs a new roof. It doesn't leak yet, but I'm afraid that with a good wind, it will. I think maybe Jeff will loan me Seth and Daniel to help with the work. It shouldn't take too long with the three of us working. I will have Clyde order the necessary building supplies so we can get started soon. I would like it to be finished by the wedding so I can walk onto the porch and pick you up and carry you over the threshold of our new home."

Valerie just grinned and gave Bill a big hug.

Chapter 8

As nasty as Anna was to them, she missed her family. Her mama and papa never had a mean word to say to her.

She did remember being spanked by her papa when she was mean to another girl in class and when she said some nasty things to Aunt Susan when she was pregnant, but he apologized afterwards.

She hadn't heard from her parents since she wrote the letter giving up custody of William to Steven and Jane. She regretted writing that letter now. She might have been able to get more out of it if she had negotiated William's custody. Unfortunately, the judge had given permanent custody to Steven and Jane. Now there wasn't much she could do to get him back.

Anna had some time coming up that was free time for her. She had worked overtime and taken the morning shift several times and she was given comp time for it.

She thought maybe she would take the train to Rawlings and see her parents. She would probably have to see William too. That she was not looking forward to. He was most likely a spoiled brat by now. She had no use for spoiled children.

Anna talked to Joe Archer about time off. He told her that the 2nd week in March was the best time. One of the boys who used to work for him was coming home for a visit and would like to earn some money. He could work Anna's shift that week.

She decided that it would be fun to surprise her parents with the visit so did not tell them she was coming. She boarded the train for Rawlings and was scheduled to arrive at 2:00 PM. on Friday, March 16, 1906.

When she got off of the train in Rawlings, she walked across the street to the hotel and found only a small staff on duty. Her parents were not there, nor were Jane or Steven.

She asked the girl at the desk where everyone was and was told that they were all at Thomas and Irene's wedding at the JSJ Ranch.

"What?" Anna exclaimed. Who was this Thomas her sister was marrying and why was she not informed, she thought.

She went out back to the livery and took a buggy that was ready to ride and went out to the ranch. Ray was over on the blacksmith side of the building and did not see who took the buggy but was ready to get on a horse and go after her.

He would have gone, but he had a horse half shod and the owner was waiting. He had to finish the job. Instead, he went to the sheriff's office and reported the buggy stolen. He thought it was a woman who took it but was not sure. He did not see her clearly.

Anna drove up to the ranch house as mad as could be that she was not informed that her sister was getting married. She stormed in the door and realized that the ceremony was just over and that it was the attorney, Thomas Campbell that Irene had married.

"What is going on here?" Anna yelled over the clapping and cheering. No one paid any attention to her, but George saw her. He rushed over to her, took her arm, and steered her back out of the front door.

"What are you doing here?" he demanded.

"I came for a visit and learned about this fiasco," Anna answered with a sneer. "I can't believe that Irene would marry that wimp of a lawyer."

George kept hold of her arm and steered her out of the door and down the stairs to the buggy that she took. "Where did you get that buggy and horse?" George asked.

"I took it from the livery. It was just sitting there and I figured it was yours and I could use it," Anna answered.

"Well, you were wrong. That buggy belongs to Judge Corbin, the judge who married Thomas and Irene. He rode out here with your Mother and me and left his buggy for Ray to repair. You are lucky you didn't break your neck driving it and you will be lucky if the judge does not press charges against you for theft of his buggy and his horse. Now, I am not going to let you spoil this day for your sister or your mother. It is a joyous occasion for all of us and you will keep your mouth shut. Do you understand that?" George said in a demanding tone.

"But why was I not informed of this wedding?" Anna pleaded.

"You were not informed because you have not seen fit to contact us in several months and we did not think you would care one way or another," George answered.

Just then, Marie came out onto the porch and saw Anna. She had a stunned look on her face and then started to cry. She had not seen her daughter in months. She wanted nothing more than to give her a big hug, but she resisted. She did not know why Anna was here and was afraid for William. He would come bounding out of the house any minute now and see her. She didn't know what his reaction would be.

William did come bounding out of the house but did not see Anna right away. He was chasing Patch who had something in his mouth he wasn't supposed to have.

Patch ran down the stairs and ran right into Anna. She was startled and kicked the dog away from her. Patch whimpered and just lay on the ground for a few minutes before he got up.

William screamed "Don't kick my dog," and ran to see if Patch was okay. When he looked up at the person who kicked Patch, he recognized his mother.

"What are you doing here?" William asked her. "You hurt my dog," said William.

"He ran right at me. I had to keep him away. Anyway, he's just a dirty old dog," Anna spit out.

"First, he's not old. He's only eight months old. Second, he isn't dirty. He had a bath today so he would be clean for the wedding, explained William. "What are you doing here?"

"None of your business. You certainly need some lessons in manners. You've changed since I had control of you," Anna said. William's only answer was to run off.

Just then, Steven and Jane came out of the house to see what all of the commotion was. When they saw Anna, they froze. "Where's William?" Jane asked.

"He ran off around the house with that stupid animal." Anna commented. "I don't know what you have done to him, but his manners are terrible. He didn't even say hello to me," Anna spit out.

"Why would he? You never paid any attention to him when he was living with you." Steven said with disgust.

Thomas and Irene came out of the front door at that time and saw Anna talking to Steven. Irene got a panicked look on her face, but Thomas assured her that William would not go with Anna. She would be charged with kidnapping if she tried to take him away.

William picked up Patch and ran down to the bunkhouse looking for Earl. He ran into the bunkhouse, slammed the door, and had a panicked look on his face.

"What's wrong William?" Earl asked.

"My mom is out there yelling at everyone and Patch ran into her and she kicked him in his side. He is walking funny now and whines when I touch the spot."

"Let's have a look," said Earl, so mad he could spit.

Earl examined Patch and thought that he was just sore and bruised from the kick. "Watch him carefully Sport and give him plenty of water to drink but be a little sparing on the food. Sometimes lots of food can cause problems with puppies' stomachs. And technically, Patch is still a puppy."

"Thanks Earl. Can I stay here for a while. I don't want to see my mother.

"Sure, you can stay here as long as you want to. Someone will be here all of the time. Isn't that right, boys?"

"Sure is!" several of the hands said.

People were coming out of the house to see what was going on. Finally, Judge Corbin walked out the door and immediately saw his buggy sitting there in front of the house.

"What is my buggy doing here?" the Judge inquired.

Anna said, "I used it to ride out here. It seems that I wasn't informed about the wedding and I wanted to be here."

"Then Mrs. Jones, you are under arrest for horse theft and theft of the Judges' buggy." Sheriff John Boyson was a guest at the wedding and happened to hear her confession. He walked down the steps and took Anna's arms and put a pair of handcuffs on her wrists. "Come with me Mrs. Jones. You are going to jail."

By this time, Anna was screaming for her mother and father to do something. They just stood there and looked at each other with regretful looks on their faces. There was nothing they could do at this time.

Anna was going to jail. She admitted taking the horse and buggy without permission.

Bill and Valerie also walked out onto the porch at the same time as Thomas and Irene did. They were surprised to see Anna standing there.

Anna was equally surprised to see Bill Kingman with her baby sister. Anna never had any great feelings for Valerie, but to see her with dirt like Billy Kingman was too much.

"Why are you standing with my sister?" Anna inquired of Bill. "You have no place here."

Susan stepped forward and said, "You have no right to say who can come into my home or not Anna Jones. Bill Kingman is a far more honorable person than you are at this moment. If you cannot be nice and have a civil tongue for my guests, you may leave. And since you stole Judge Corbin's horse and buggy, you really don't have any rights at all.

Anna spun around and muttered to the sheriff, "get me out of here." The sheriff obliged and put her in the back of his buggy.

"I guess I will drive my own buggy back to town. Someone follow me in case it breaks down. I don't think the blacksmith had a chance to fix it before Mrs. Jones took it," mentioned Judge Corbin.

Irene looked at Susan with love and gratitude. "Thank you so much for a lovely day. I am so grateful to have a family like I have, even if one member is a little wacky. We will see you in a couple of weeks."

Thomas and Irene had thought that they would wait until school was out in June before they took their honeymoon but decided to go ahead and go now. Fiona Stephens had agreed to teach the class for Irene during the time she was gone.

Irene and Thomas would be staying in her house near the school until her parents left for the Oregon Coast. Then they would move into George and Marie's house. Earl was going to take the time to remodel it for them and build a separate entrance for clients. As soon as it was ready, Thomas would move his office down from Colfax.

As everyone was leaving, William came around the corner of the house with Patch. Patch was still sore from the kick that Anna had given him, but he had no permanent damage. William was very angry at his mother and did not ever want to see her again. He was very glad he walked away from her. He probably would have said something he would have later regretted saying.

He knew that people were supposed to respect their mothers. Irene, Charlotte, Freddie, and Valerie respected their mother. He respected his grandmother, but not his mother. She did not seem to do anything to earn his respect.

People were packing up to go home. It was a lovely wedding until Anna spoiled it, but Thomas and Irene were not letting anything harm their wedding day. They were looking forward to two weeks together with no one to bother them. They would be back just in time for Bill and Valerie's wedding.

As Steven was driving their buggy out of the stable and getting ready to help Jane up onto the seat, William asked, "Why does my mother hate everyone?"

Steven answered him with "None of us know William. We think something happened when she was young and it affected the way she felt about herself. Your mother always wants to be the center of attention and it makes her very angry when she isn't. It is a disease William and unless she wants to get help, there is not much we can do about it."

Blake and Fiona Stephens were riding back to town with Bill and Valerie. Fiona was going to substitute for Irene while she was on her honeymoon. The main topic of conversation of course, was Anna and the spectacle she made of herself on Susan's front porch.

The ladies were sitting in the back seat of the buggy and Blake and Bill were sitting in the front. They were busy talking about the farm that Bill and Valerie were buying and what upgrades needed to be done before they could move in. It was just a short time until their wedding and they wanted it to be ready to move in when they got back from their 2-week honeymoon. They were going to go camping. They would take a wagon with a cover on it along with horses to pull it and go into the mountains of Northern Idaho and up to a lake that Bill had heard of. It was supposed to have the best fishing around and they both loved to fish.

They also liked to eat the fish that they caught and were looking forward to fresh lake trout suppers cooked over an open fire.

"Fiona and I think that sounds pretty good. We also like the fresh fish cooked over an open fire. Maybe we will join you on this fishing trip. Let's ask Susan if she will come into town and teach for a couple of weeks," Blake said as he was laughing at the looks on their faces. "Blake, you are scaring this lovely young couple. Stop teasing them," Fiona ordered. "They do not know you well enough to know when you are teasing or being serious."

When the sheriff got Anna back to the jail, he sat her down in a chair and looked at her. He knew she must be scared, but she didn't show it.

"Now young lady, you tell me why I shouldn't throw you into jail and keep you there. Do you know that you could be hanged for stealing a horse," he said with a commanding voice.

Sheriff John Boyson was normally a very mild-mannered man. He didn't get riled up about many things, but this situation with Anna Seevers Jones made him mad. Here was a lovely young lady who was ruining her life with her words and actions. Now she had the audacity to steal a horse. Not just any horse, but Judge Corbin's horse. He didn't want to lock her up, but he really didn't have a choice at this point. She had admitted stealing the horse. Granted, she hadn't said she stole the horse, she said she took it, but it was the same thing. She took what did not belong to her.

"At this point, Mrs. Jones, I do not have a choice but to put you in a cell for the night. You admitted to the crime of horse theft and you admitted it in front of Judge Corbin, whose horse you stole," explained the sheriff.

"I just wanted to get out to the ranch. My family was all out there and I was upset because they hadn't informed me that my sister was getting married. I would have liked to be there for the ceremony. My son was there also and I haven't seen him in several months," Anna pleaded.

"I have a note here on my desk that says, 'Do not let Anna Jones anywhere near her son William Jones without someone being with him. She is in no way allowed to see him alone or remove him from Rawlings, Washington. That note has been on my desk for several months. It is my understanding that you have not tried to contact him since you voluntarily gave up custody of him," added Sheriff Boyson.

"Since you gave up custody of your son and obviously do not have much of an interest in your sisters or brother and with your parents moving away from Rawlings, you will not have reason to return if I put you on a train back to Lewiston, will you?" asked the sheriff.

"What do you mean, my parents are leaving Rawlings!" cried Anna. "They would never leave this town. They love it here. This is their home!"

"They are moving right after your sister Valerie gets married next month. They are moving to Cannon Beach, Oregon," Sheriff Boyson said.

"First of all, Valerie is making a big mistake marrying that Kingman trash. The whole family is rotten. And I can't believe that my parents would ever sell the hotel," said Anna.

"They are not selling. They are handing over the management to your brother. He is a fine young man and extremely capable of running the hotel," said the sheriff.

"That is ridiculous! He is way too young. I could do a much better job of running the hotel than that silly little boy could. I will talk to them about turning it over to me instead," Anna said with authority in her voice and dollar signs in her eyes. "My father will do anything for me," she stated firmly.

"You are dreaming young lady. The deed is done and it has been done legally. The papers are signed. I even witnessed them for Judge Corbin. So, you might as well get that idea out of your head. Anyway, you will not have a chance to do much of anything from a jail cell."

Sheriff Boyson stood up and directed Anna to stand and walk towards the jail cell. He had no other choice but to lock her up for the night.

"You are not really going to put me in that filthy cell are you?" Anna pleaded.

"That's where you are headed for the night, Mrs. Jones." Sheriff Boyson said.

"But, I have to get back to Lewiston to go to work tomorrow," Anna cried.

"You should have thought of that before you stole Judge Corbin's horse and buggy," Sheriff Boyson said.

Judge Corbin drove his horse and buggy back to Rawlings. He was in the lead of a caravan of buggies and wagons coming back to town from the JSJ Ranch and Irene and Thomas Campbell's wedding.

The Judge was fuming all the way back about Anna Jones taking his horse and buggy. She could have been seriously hurt. The buggy needed some work on one of the wheels and it was not really safe to drive.

What was he going to do about Anna Jones? She really made a fool of herself at the ranch. She scared her son when she kicked his dog. She did not even greet her parents nicely.

She should be punished for her actions today, but on the other hand, she had only harmed herself. He could put her on the train back to Lewiston and forbid her to come to Rawlings again. If she did, she would be arrested and sent to prison as a horse thief. Yes, that is what he would do. But she could spend tonight in jail instead of a nice soft bed in the hotel. He would talk to John Boyson in the morning.

George and Marie were beside themselves with worry about their daughter. They knew that she would spend the night in a jail cell, but there was nothing much they could do about her situation. She had admitted to taking the horse from the livery.

Their daughter, Anna Seevers Jones, was a horse thief. The idea made them both shudder.

"Do you suppose they would let us see her tomorrow?" Marie asked.

"I really don't know if I want to see her Marie," George said. "She had such a cruel, twisted look on her face. She didn't look like our Anna at all. And I am worried about William's reaction to all of this. What is it going to do to him?"

"Maybe it's best if we don't see her, but she is our little girl and we are moving away. We might never see her again," Marie thought out loud.

"Let's get some rest tonight. We will go to the jail tomorrow to see her and to see what will happen to her," George said as he helped her into the house and took her coat for her.

Marie missed Charlotte. She could not make it to the wedding because of school. She attended the Sacred Heart School of Nursing in Spokane, WA. She was in her last year of school on her way to becoming an operating room nurse. She would graduate in June and then have to take the State of Washington exam to become a licensed operating room nurse.

George and Marie were so proud of her for sticking to her dream of becoming a nurse. She had been gone from home for almost four years now, but they still missed her terribly.

Both George and Marie had high hopes for all of their children. All but Anna had never disappointed them. Irene had been an excellent teacher and had just entered into a good marriage with Thomas. Freddie was going to make a great manager of the hotel. He took to the business right away and was very quick at grasping all of the facets of running a successful hotel. He wasn't much of a cook, but that's what Jim Barnes was for and he was a great cook. Valerie was going to make a beautiful bride and be a great wife and mother. That is all she ever wanted to do.

George and Marie were convinced that Bill Kingman would make a good husband for Valerie. Despite his upbringing by his father, he was a good man and cared deeply for his mother, brothers, and sisters and for Valerie. He would make a great success of his farm.

Then there was Anna. She was such a worry for them, but they did not want her situation to hinder their move to Oregon. Both of them were looking forward to a new adventure.

Judge Corbin walked over to the sheriff's office the next morning. John Boyson was sitting at his desk drinking a cup of coffee. He looked like he had not slept all night.

"You look terrible John," stated the judge.

"I feel terrible. I didn't sleep all night. Mrs. Jones either screamed, yelled, or threatened bodily harm to everyone who lives in Rawlings all night. No one could have slept through all that noise. She finally wore herself out about five o'clock this morning. By that time, I was so hyped up on coffee, I couldn't go to sleep," stated John.

"Have you thought what you want to do with her?" asked the Judge.

"I'm not sure. I would like to throttle her, but that would be against the law. I was thinking about putting her on the train to Lewiston and telling her not to return to Rawlings. If she did, she would be subject to arrest and trial for horse theft. What do you think?" asked John.

"That sounds okay to me. I really don't want to send her to prison. Hopefully a night in jail will teach her a lesson," Judge Corbin said.

"I doubt it!" answered John, sarcastically.

About that time, George and Marie walked into the office. They wanted to see Anna but weren't sure whether she would want to see them.

"Good morning George, Marie," John greeted them. "I suppose you want to see your daughter?"

"We would like to, but does she want to see us?" George asked.

"She probably does. She has been yelling and screaming and asking for you most of the night," explained John.

"Papa, I hear you out there. Get me out of here right now," screamed Anna.

"You stay here for a minute sweetheart. Let me talk to her for a few minutes," George said to Marie.

Marie sat down in a chair while George went in to see Anna.

"Papa, get me out of here right now. I should never have been left in here. I expected you to come and get me last night. Why didn't you?" Anna asked.

"First of all, you deserved to be here last night. You stole Judge Corbin's horse and buggy. That is a very serious offense. Do you know that horse stealing is still a hanging offense in this state?" George asked. "What makes you think that I want to get you out of jail when you speak to me the way you just did? For the first time, I can honestly say that I am ashamed of you," "Your mother and I are leaving right after

Valerie and Bill's wedding and moving to Cannon Beach, Oregon. If we come back to this area at all, it will be for a visit only. It is my understanding from the Sheriff that you will not be welcome in Rawlings anymore. If you do come back, you could be arrested for horse theft," George continued to explain to his daughter. "Your mother would like to see you, but if you do anything or say anything to upset her, I will request that you stand trial. Do you understand?" George asked.

"Yes!" Anna said, with very little meaning in her voice.

George went back out to the office to let Marie know that she could go in and see Anna.

Marie was very quiet as she went in. She looked at Anna and started crying again. All she could say was "Why?"

"I don't know why Mama. I was mad that no one had told me that Irene was getting married. Why in the world did she marry that wimpy attorney?" Anna asked.

"Thomas is not wimpy. He is a very good attorney, makes a very good living and loves your sister. She loves him. Why would you begrudge her happiness? She has done nothing at all to harm you," Marie explained.

"You kept having more babies Mama. I wanted to be your only child. I wanted all of your attention and you couldn't, nor would you give me the attention I needed," said Anna.

"That is so selfish. We loved all of you equally. We didn't give any of you more love and attention than the others. Sometimes, one or the other of you needed some additional attention due to special circumstances, but we always tried to make up that time," explained Marie. Your father and I are leaving right after Valerie and Bill are married in April. We will be moving to Cannon Beach, Oregon," Marie told her.

"Papa told me. I think that I could do a better job of running the hotel than Freddie. You should have turned it over to me, being the oldest child," Anna complained.

"That is the most ridiculous thing I have ever heard," Marie laughed.

Anna just looked at her with a pained expression on her face and said, "Goodbye Mama!"

Marie left the room and walked out to George and they left to get some fresh air outside.

CHAPTER 9

Bill Kingman and Valerie Seevers were married on April 21, 1906, at the Rawlings Christian Church. George Seevers walked his daughter down the aisle and gave her to Bill with gratitude and love, knowing that Bill would take care of his baby girl.

Virginia Rodgers sat in the front pew with tears streaming down her face. She was so proud of Bill for becoming the fine young man that he was and overcoming such a fractured childhood. She hoped that he would always be as happy as he was today.

Marie was in tears watching Charlotte walk down the aisle as Valerie's maid of honor and then George walking Valerie down the aisle.

The church was full of people there to celebrate the joyful day. Thomas and Irene were back from their honeymoon. Irene looked radiant as a new wife. She was doubly excited because the school board was going to let her continue to teach, not just until the end of the school year in June, but next fall also.

William was disappointed that Patch couldn't come to the wedding. Patch stayed home by himself. The church didn't like having dogs inside. He was also afraid that his mother might show up like she did at Irene and Thomas' wedding.

There were several people concerned about Anna showing up, Sheriff Boyson for one. He was on the alert for any signs of trouble.

George did his last baking in the hotel kitchen for Valerie's wedding reception. He baked a beautiful wedding cake for his daughter and her new husband.

The reception was held in the hotel lobby. There weren't many outside guests at the hotel that weekend, but the ones that were staying there were welcome to join the reception and have some cake and coffee.

Virginia's children were there in force to celebrate their brother and his new wife. All of them were concerned that somehow their father, Otis would cause trouble. He was still in prison, but he could have influence on the outside.

Otis had been in prison now for 19 years. He had originally been sentenced to 3 years but had been in a fight and caused the death of another inmate. Because of that and the fact that his method of settling arguments was to fight, his sentence was extended several times to a total of 20 years.

Otis had finally figured out that he needed to have a good record in prison in order to be released at the end of his 20 years. He was determined that he was going back to Rawlings and getting his wife and family and farm back. Some crooked lawyer wasn't going to tell him that Virginia was not his wife and that his farm was sold. Mousy little Virginia would not have had the nerve to sell the farm.

Seth, Daniel, and Bill were grown now and would be able to do the work needed to make the farm successful. Someday, he would buy enough land to have a ranch, not just a farm. Virginia and the girls would take care of him the way he should be taken care of.

In the meantime, he would do everything the way he was supposed to so that he would be released in the fall of 1906.

James Kingman was 17 years old and working with Clyde in the General Store. He was learning the business very quickly and would be able to take over the management of the store in a few years when Clyde and Virginia wanted to retire.

Virginia was basking in the attention and kindness that Clyde showed to her. She had never before had the attention or the love that Clyde gave to her.

Clyde in turn was overwhelmed at the love that Virginia had for him. She took care of him like he was a jewel in a crown. As far as she was concerned, he was.

Business at the store was brisk. Clyde, with James' help was doing a great job of keeping the store shelves stocked with merchandise that the customers wanted. Before James started working there, Clyde had a hard time anticipating what customers would want and would buy. James seemed to instinctively know what people would want and ordered appropriately.

Clyde was impressed with James' ability to know the customers wants. He knew who baked on what day and if they needed sugar or flour for their baking. He seemed to have the ability to anticipate the needs of the customers, unlike Clyde.

When it was time for James to take over, Clyde knew that the business would be in good hands.

Even though Virginia was blissfully happy with Clyde, she was always on edge because of Otis. She realized that his 20-year sentence would be up in October and he could be out of prison. She was sure he would return to Rawlings and she was afraid of what he would do to the children and her. He would probably hurt Clyde too.

All of the children were aware of Otis' possible release and were on alert. They also assumed that he would return to Rawlings. Now that Bill had married Valerie, that put her in peril also. No one was sure what he would do.

Sheriff John Boyson had asked to be notified if and when Otis was released from prison. There was no way that he could prevent him from coming back to Rawlings, but he would keep very close track of him if he did come back.

John kept a tight rein on the town. Occasionally there would be an instance where someone from one of the saloons next to the railroad depot would cause a problem and have to sober up in jail overnight, but he did not have to arrest too many people.

Rawlings was a quiet town and the citizens generally got along well. There was a lot of respect for each other. Most of the people who lived in Rawlings attributed the quiet, peaceful town to the influence of George and Marie Seevers. Collectively, they were the anchor that kept the town together. People were concerned about the direction that the town would take without the Seevers leaving there.

George and Marie were ready to move to Cannon Beach, Oregon. On May 1, 1906, the town of Rawlings gave them a going away party. They all crowded into the schoolhouse to wish them well and to say goodbye.

"I want to thank all of you so much on behalf of Marie and myself. We have made this town our home for 22 years and we have loved every minute of it. It is hard to remember what it looked like when we first moved here. There was no store, bank, church, sheriff's office, or a doctor's office, and half the homes in town are new since then. The hotel, schoolhouse and railroad station were about the only buildings in town. We have made some lifelong friends here and our children grew up here. Rawlings will always have a place in our hearts, but the Pacific Ocean and especially Cannon Beach is our dream. The Ocean was my quest for almost my whole life and the few days I spent there when William was born were not enough to satisfy that longing," George told the crowd.

Marie, as usual, had tears streaming down her face. It would be hard for both of them to leave, but it was time for a new adventure and their children were capable of taking care of themselves.

Both George and Marie were hoping to see Judge Corbin again to thank him for being lenient with Anna in March, but he had a full work load for the months of April and May and could not get to

Rawlings. He did send a telegram and wished them a successful trip and a happy retirement.

Just before they left the schoolhouse, William came up to them and asked if he could come and visit them sometime. That statement made Marie's heart soar.

"You absolutely can come to visit. You could even come and spend the summer if you wanted to," Marie said.

"Could Patch come too?" asked William.

"Remember, where you go Patch goes. Of course, he can come! I know for sure that he can ride on the train. I have seen dogs get off of the train many times," George answered.

Some of the citizens were concerned about the direction the town would take with George and Marie gone. Rawlings had never had a city government. Maybe it was time to think about forming one.

Thomas Campbell would be the logical person to contact about forming a government and having an election. Probably another town meeting was in order to discuss the possibilities.

Thomas Campbell, Jeff Jordan, Blake Stephens, Freddie Seevers, and Steven Taylor met in the hotel restaurant for lunch one day to discuss the date for a town meeting and an agenda to follow. All five of them knew that the topic of politics and government could be volatile and they wanted to head off as much argument as possible.

June 8, 1906, was the date set for the town meeting. Notices were posted all over town about the meeting. A potluck supper would be held just before.

June 8th turned out to be a beautiful day so tables were set up outside of the schoolhouse for the potluck supper. There was a lot of speculation as to what the meeting would be about and rumors were flying. When supper was over, most of the people moved into the school for the meeting.

Jeff Jordan got up and introduced everyone seated in front, Thomas Campbell, Blake Stephens, Freddie Seevers, and Steven Taylor.

"I believe in this town and I believe that we can do great things in this area of Washington, but I do think we need some direction. We have asked for this meeting to explore the possibility of forming a city government with a mayor and city council. Since the city would have no money to pay a mayor, it would have to be a voluntary job," explained Jeff.

"Because we do not have any money to provide any services, property taxes would have to be assessed. They would be minimal and would be paid to a city treasurer."

Thomas got up to speak then. "All of this would have to be worked out. Really, the purpose of this meeting is to investigate the possibility of forming a city government and to see what you, as the citizens of this town think about the idea."

"Right now, what government control we have in this city comes from the County of Columbia, which is situated in Dayton, an overnight train ride away from here. The taxes that we pay to Columbia

County go for services all over the county and do not always benefit Rawlings. I don't want to pay extra taxes either, but I do want what I pay to benefit the town in which I live," stated Steven.

"How would we choose the officers of the city?" someone hollered from the back of the room.

Jeff explained, "We would have an election. People would declare themselves as a candidate for a specific office and campaign for that office. A specific date would be chosen for the election of the officers."

Blake got up to explain the officers, "We would need candidates for Mayor, maybe 3 or 4 councilmen, a city treasurer, and a city auditor to begin with. If someone feels that they want to run for that job, then they will declare themselves a candidate for that office and start campaigning for it."

"How will we know that the candidates are honest and won't try to rip us off?" someone else asked.

"I have agreed to do a thorough background check on each candidate. That background check will tell us if that person has ever been in jail and what for," Thomas explained. "Being an attorney in the State of Washington, I have the ability to do these types of checks."

"I think it is a good idea. Let's do it!" Someone else yelled out.

"Is there anyone else who would like to be on the committee to set up this election?" Jeff asked.

"Yes, I would like to help," Bill Kingman said.

"Do we need a jailbird's son working on this?" another man hollered from the back of the room.

"Bill Kingman is one of the nicest, most honest men I have ever met. He worked for me for a lot of years and did an excellent job. He is starting out with his own farm now and is doing an excellent job of running it. He deserves a chance just like anyone else. His father has nothing to do with this," Jeff Jordan said with authority in his voice.

No one else commented.

Susan, Irene, Fiona, Valerie, and Virginia were all out at the farm working on election posters. They would be posted all over town notifying people when to announce their candidacy for office, where to sign up and what office they were seeking.

William and some of his friends from school took the posters and nailed them to every building and light pole and telephone pole in town. Their instructions were to make sure they asked the building owners permission before they nailed them to their building.

The boys made a game of it to see who could get rid of their posters the fastest.

Bill Kingman was eager to become involved in the community. He and Valerie attended church every Sunday and were becoming involved with the activities of the church.

Valerie had volunteered to teach a Sunday School class for the pre-school children. Her parents had always gone to church and involved their children in the activities. Valerie felt very comfortable in church. Bill was a little more hesitant about becoming involved. He had never been inside the church until he started going out with Valerie. His father did not believe in going to church and would not allow his wife or children to attend.

With Valerie by his side, Bill was becoming more comfortable though and was becoming acquainted with many of the people who lived in Rawlings that he had never met before.

Moreover, the citizens of Rawlings were becoming aware that Bill Kingman was nothing like his father. They were learning that he was a very polite well-spoken young man and was very intelligent. Even though he had a late start on his formal education because of his fathers' restrictions, he learned very quickly and was eager to be a part of the new government of Rawlings.

It was the consensus of the men who called for the town meeting, that the election should be held on the second Tuesday of November 1906 and that the term of office for each person elected would be four years.

There were three men running for Mayor: Steven Taylor, Earl Jansen, foreman of JSJ Ranch and Ray Clausen, blacksmith. All three were well qualified to be Mayor. They had lived in the area for many years and were acquainted with most of the citizens of Rawlings.

Bill Kingman and Freddie Seevers were too young to be mayor of the town but were running for a city council seat. Clyde Rodgers was running for city treasurer and Blake Stephens was running for county auditor. The only election that was contested was that of Mayor. All of the other offices had no opponent, so would win the seat.

All summer there were speeches and lunches and get togethers to talk about the election and who would be the best candidate for mayor of Rawlings. The three candidates decided to have a debate about the issues that faced the city and what needed to be done to improve services to the citizens.

Friday September 7,1906 was the date chosen for the debate. Thomas Campbell acted as moderator of the debate and questions were submitted by the public. All three candidates had lived in Rawlings for a long time and knew the town and most of its citizens well and their views were similar on what was needed for the town to grow. The questions came down to how each man would handle certain situations that arose.

Most everyone thought the debate was very interesting but didn't help them make up their minds as to who would make the best mayor. It came down to who they liked best.

People who had lived in Rawlings for a long time were aware that Otis Kingman was due to be released from prison sometime in October 1906. John Boyson, the sheriff had advised everyone to be on the alert for him. Otis had continuously said that he was coming back to Rawlings and his wife and family. Virginia legally sold the farm in March of 1888 to Bruce Williams. Bruce had the farm next door to the Kingman farm and had since made a big success of raising poultry on the expanding farm along with growing some wheat and corn. There was no distinction between the two farms now. The Kingman house and outbuildings had been torn down and the land plowed for growing corn.

Otis believed that he still owned the farm and was liable to cause major problems when he realized that it wasn't his anymore. He had always been a violent man and that was his way of solving problems.

Clyde was growing afraid for Virginia and her children and very rarely left her alone when she was not working. Virginia loved her job as head of housekeeping at the hotel. The cleanliness of the rooms and common areas had never been as good before Virginia started working, but she was always on edge for fear that Otis would walk into the hotel, and she would have to see him.

On October 16, 1906, Otis Kingman was released from prison in Walla Walla, Washington. He had served his 20-year sentence. He had $20.00 in his pocket, one dollar for every year he had served. The first thing he did was head for a bar and bought himself a glass of whiskey.

After he drank the glass of whiskey, he headed for the train station and bought a ticket to Rawlings. He was going home!

The warden at the Walla Walla state prison had contacted the sheriff of Rawlings, John Boysen and let him know that Otis was released on Tuesday the 16th and was likely on his way to Rawlings.

Sheriff Boysen walked over to the hotel to see Virginia. He found her in the lobby talking to Steven and Jane. "Hi!" he greeted all three of them. "Can we step into your office for a minute Steven?" They moved into Steven's office quickly. "I wanted to let you know that I have heard from the warden at the prison that Otis has been released from prison. He feels that it is likely that he will be coming here."

Virginia slumped down in a chair. "Please let Clyde and all of the children know," she begged. "I am truly afraid for all of them. Nothing will be the same for him and he will be very angry when he finds out that we are not available for him. I don't know what he will do."

"The first train from Walla Walla is due here in two hours. I will be at the depot when it comes in. I have never met the man, but I have a picture of him," explained the sheriff. "Your family will be informed of his release as will Blake Stephens. I understand he had some trouble with him also."

"Yes he did," said Virginia. "When my baby died, Dr. Stephens found me and confronted Otis about it. Otis said some nasty things to the doctor."

"You try and relax," John Boyson said smiling at Virginia. "You might want to go home and be with your husband. I know he is worried about you."

"Thanks sheriff, "Virginia said.

"Thanks John. We will be on the alert," commented Steven.

John Boyson left the hotel and walked across the street to the train depot. "Is the train from Walla Walla on time?" John asked Pete Bailey, the new dispatcher.

"Right on time as usual," Pete said.

Peter Bailey was a short, rotund man about 50 years old. He had worked for the railroad for 20 years and had been a dispatcher for the last 10 years. He and his wife had moved to Rawlings 3 months ago and hoped that this would be their last job before retirement. They both liked the city and the people. Lydia Bailey was a welcome addition to the community. She immediately joined the ladies group at the Christian Church and was a welcome addition to the library area in the hotel lobby.

"Pete, I am watching for a man coming from Walla Walla named Otis Kingman. He has just been released from prison and is more than likely to come back to Rawlings. His sons are here and Virginia Rodgers is his ex-wife. He does not accept the fact that he is divorced from Virginia and that he no longer has a farm in the area. He is liable to cause trouble," explained John.

"I know the Kingman boys. They are fine young men," said Pete. "I will keep an eye out for the fellow."

"Thanks Pete!" said John.

Sheriff Boysen sat down on a bench in the waiting room of the depot. He pulled his hat down over his forehead so he could observe the arriving passengers without being obvious.

The train from Walla Walla pulled into the Rawlings station on time. There were seven passengers to get off of the train; a husband and wife and their four children were the first off. The children were all anxious to get off and move around.

The last passenger off of the train was Otis Kingman. Sheriff Boyson recognized him right away. He had the pallor of someone who had been in prison. He looked around the platform expecting to see his family waiting for him. When he didn't see anyone, he got a very angry look on his face.

"Otis Kingman?" Sheriff Boysen said as he approached Otis.

"Yea, that's me," Otis answered. "What do you want?" Otis answered as he turned around and saw the Sheriff's badge pinned to the sheriff's jacket. His face took on a suspicious expression as he stood there. "I done nothing wrong. Don't hassle me," Otis commanded.

John looked at Otis and said, "There is nothing for you here Mr. Kingman. You might as well get back onto the train and head away from Rawlings. We do not want any trouble in this town."

"I ain't going to cause no trouble. My wife and boys are here and I have a farm to look after," explained Otis.

"You have an ex-wife Mr. Kingman. She divorced you shortly after you went to prison," said John.

Otis started yelling at John, saying that he had a wife and no judge was going to tell him that they were not married anymore.

"Let me assure you Mr. Kingman, you do not have a wife and your children do not want to see you. If you do anything to cause any trouble to any of them, you will find yourself in my jail and soon back in prison in Walla Walla."

"I'm just takin back what's mine," Otis insisted. "Ain't nothin' wrong with that!"

"The problem for you Otis, is it's not yours. The farm was sold, your wife divorced you when you went to prison and your kids don't want to see you," reiterated Sheriff Boyson.

Otis just looked at him with an evil grin and left the train depot. Sheriff Boyson followed him to see where he was headed. He walked toward what used to be his farm.

Bruce Williams was the Kingman's neighbor. He never got along with Otis and they constantly had arguments about property lines and animals encroaching on Otis' property. When Otis went to prison and Virginia decided to sell the farm and move further into town, Bruce Williams offered to buy it. He wanted to expand his own property and the Kingman property was perfect.

As Otis approached what used to be his property, all he saw was a field of dried-up corn stalks ready to be plowed under. Otis just stood and stared. Where was his house and barn? Where were the fences that were around his farm? Where was his family?

Otis saw a man in the adjoining field with horses hooked up to a plow. He climbed over the fence to talk to the man. Something was definitely wrong. His farm couldn't have just disappeared, but it had

Bruce Williams saw the man coming across his field and knew that it was Otis Kingman. He knew by the man's walk and the anger that was evident in the way he was walking.

"Stop right there Kingman!" Williams said. "You are trespassing on my property."

"This ain't your property. It's mine and always has been. No one had the right to sell it without my okay and I didn't okay it. You are trespassing on my property."

"No! I have a signed bill of sale that is recorded in the county office in Dayton. It is my property and has been for 19 years. Now, get off!" ordered Williams.

Otis stood there for a moment and realized that there was nothing he could do right then, but he would get that woman and make her get his farm back for him. He turned around and stomped off across the field.

Bruce took the horses and plow back to the barn and went into his house to call Sheriff Boyson.

"Sheriff, Otis Kingman was just here talking up a storm about getting his property back. I am afraid for Virginia and her children. He muttered something about finding that woman and making her get his property back."

"Thanks Bruce for letting me know. Was he on foot or riding a horse?" the sheriff asked.

"He was on foot so it will take him a little time to get back to town. He is a very angry man and that makes him dangerous Sheriff. You take care and get help if you need it," Bruce mentioned.

"Thanks Bruce. Talk to you later."

Chapter 10

Sheriff John Boyson was aware of almost everything that went on in Rawlings. He was very aware of the impact that Otis's return was having on the city. Clyde and Virginia were on high alert as were all the Kingman children.

Seth and Daniel both worked at the JSJ Ranch but had come into town to stay with their mother and stepfather for a while. Neither Josephine nor Margaret lived in Rawlings. Josephine was a nurse in a hospital in Cheyenne, Wyoming and Margaret taught at a school in Spokane. Bill and Valerie were living on their farm just outside of Rawlings and were aware that Otis was in town. Bill was not sure that Otis would remember what he looked like.

James worked at the store with Clyde, but he was pretty sure that Otis would not recognize him. He still walked with a limp caused by Otis when James was a child but had grown tall and had grown a beard which has helped to disguise his appearance.

Sheriff Boyson thought he might need some help if things were to get out of hand with Otis. He asked Ray Clausen to become a temporary deputy sheriff for some backup in case the situation turned violent.

Both Seth and Daniel have volunteered to patrol the town to keep track of Otis. Virginia had been asked to remain in the hotel, preferably out of sight for the time being.

Otis didn't appear back in town until Friday, October 19TH. No one was sure where he was on the night of the 18th, but Sheriff Boyson saw him walk across the street from the saloon to go into the dining room at the hotel.

George Seevers had always made a habit of denying service to anyone who was obviously drunk, and Freddie Seevers continued that policy. When he denied a table to Otis, Otis became enraged and started turning tables over and throwing chairs around the room. Then he pulled a gun on Freddie. The sheriff saw him pull the gun and grabbed his arm before he could fire it. Otis was struggling and swearing at Freddie and the sheriff, but the sheriff managed to get a pair of handcuffs on him and haul him over to the jail.

"I am sorry folks," Freddie said to the other customers in the dining room. "I am paying for your meals because of the commotion. This is not a normal occurrence in the hotel or in Rawlings. Please, I hope you can relax and enjoy the rest of your meal."

Most of the diners were passing through town on the train and had stopped for a noon meal before continuing on to Portland. They were all scared when Otis came in and were very impressed at the way in which the sheriff and Freddie defused the situation so quickly. And the fact that their meals were paid for made them very happy.

As soon as John Boyson got Otis locked into a cell, he called the hotel to let Virginia know that Otis was locked up again.

"Otis went out to the Williams place and accused Bruce of trespassing on his property then apparently spent the night drinking in the saloon. He went into the dining room at the hotel and pulled a gun on Freddie for refusing him service. I was able to get the gun away from him and lock him up," John explained to Virginia. "You should be safe now."

"Because Otis was released from prison for completing his sentence, he will have to go through a trial on the charges of being a felon with a gun, disturbing the peace and threatening bodily harm on someone," John explained to Virginia.

John called Judge Albert Corbin and explained the situation to him. "I will come down in a couple of days to set a hearing and/or trial date," the judge explained. "Keep him locked up until then. There will be no bail for him now."

Otis passed out the minute he sat down on the bunk in the jail cell. He had probably been up most of the night before, drinking at the saloon. When he woke up in the morning, he started yelling at the sheriff to let him out of jail. He didn't know why he was there in the first place.

"You were drunk and you had a gun. You went into the hotel dining room and pulled out a gun intending to shoot someone. That is against the law!" explained the sheriff. Where did you get the gun Otis?"

"I don't know. Probably won it in a poker game. What's wrong with me having a gun. I need to defend myself," answered Otis. "Now, let me out of this cell. I need to find my family and get my farm back."

"Otis, I don't know how many times we have to tell you. You do not have a farm anymore. It was sold by your ex-wife after she divorced you and moved into town. You no longer have a family Otis. You might have children, but you do not have a family. They do not want to see you."

"Well, I want to see them. Get them in here now!" Otis yelled.

"No! I will not get them in here. I will not subject them to your verbal abuse. Just sit down and be quiet. Maybe I can get you some breakfast," the sheriff told him.

"Get me a drink!" demanded Otis.

"You know better than that. You cannot drink while you are in jail. Grow up Otis. You are not accepting reality. Judge Corbin will be in town tomorrow. You are going to face charges of destruction of property and threatening Freddie Seevers with a gun. There are a lot of witnesses against you and you probably will not beat the charges. It would be to your advantage to take responsibility for what you did and plead guilty," lectured the sheriff.

"I did nothing wrong. I was just trying to get my property and my family back and I was hungry and wanted something to eat. They would not serve me," Otis continued to insist.

"Otis, the hotel dining room has never served anyone who is obviously drunk and you were very drunk. The have the right to not provide you with service. Be sensible Otis. You were in the wrong. And I will say again, you do not own any property in Rawlings or the surrounding area. Virginia sold the property after she divorced you. It belongs to Bruce Williams now."

"No! That is wrong. Mousy little Virginia would not have had the nerve to divorce me or sell the farm. She couldn't even cook a decent meal for me, let alone understand anything about divorce or selling property," screamed Otis. "No! No! No!"

Finally, Sheriff Boyson closed the door between his office and the cells and tried to block out Otis's screaming and yelling. He figured he would get tired after a while and calm down.

Both Seth and Daniel Kingman were relieved when they were told that their father was back in jail. Virginia had told them about the incident in the dining room and about the gun being pointed towards Freddie. They were anxious to get back out to the ranch. Both boys were valued employees of the JSJ Ranch and had lived and worked there for almost 20 years. Neither one of them had ever had a girlfriend or been to a dance or had any social life except for what was on the ranch. They were perfectly happy being cowboys.

Seth and Daniel had never gone to school until their father went to prison, then Susan Jordan tutored them at the ranch. They both turned out to be very intelligent young men and were avid readers. They would occasionally come into town and get books from the small library in the lobby of the hotel and Susan gave them total access to her extensive library. They could carry on an intelligent conversation on any number of topics.

"Daniel lets head home," Seth said. "I don't think Pop will be a danger to Mama now. She sounded pretty relieved when I talked to her. Earl will be needing us to make sure the cattle are in their winter pasture."

"I'm ready anytime you are. Let's stop by the hotel and say goodbye to Mama and then head out," answered Daniel. "Do you want to see Pop?" he asked Seth.

"No! I don't think it is a good idea for him to see us. We have both changed a lot in 20 years and I don't want him to know what we look like. He doesn't need to know what Bill or James or the girls look like either," Seth answered.

They packed their extra stuff in their saddlebags, saddled their horses and were off to the hotel to say goodbye to their mama.

"Thank you boys for coming and staying with us. We do appreciate your time away from the ranch," Virginia said with tears running down her cheeks. "I am so proud of you boys and what you have accomplished in the last 20 years. I know you are happy at the ranch and that matters to me."

"Thanks mama! We will see you when we come in to vote on the 13th," said Seth.

The boys mounted their horses and rode out towards the ranch. Virginia stood on the porch of the hotel looking at them and thanking God for giving her the strength to give them up to the Jordan's 20 years ago. They were able to learn to read and write and do honest jobs on the ranch and she was very thankful for that. They were good boys!

Judge Albert Corbin arrived in Rawlings from Colfax on Thursday, November 1, 1906. He brought his wife Audrey with him. He had talked about Rawlings so much when he was here for the custody hearing for William Jones that she wanted to see the town. Audrey was intrigued by small towns and Albert had talked so much about the people who lived here and how they were so invested in their town and its residents.

The judge also brought along Simon Jacobs a young lawyer who would represent Otis. "Otis has been accused of brandishing a gun at Freddie Seevers and being drunk and disorderly so he does deserve to have a lawyer represent him," the judge explained.

Jane Taylor checked them into the hotel. She was delighted to see Judge Corbin again and to meet his wife.

"I do hope you have a pleasant stay in Rawlings," Jane told them. "Mrs. Corbin, if you need anything while the judge is working, please let me know. I will be happy to help you. We do have a very nice dining room here in the hotel and we serve tea every afternoon at 4:00 PM. I would love to have you join me," Jane asked hopefully.

"I would love to join you for tea. When Albert gets busy with his cases, he kind of forgets about anything else, including me," Audrey said with a chuckle and loving look at her husband.

"I can never forget about you my dear," he answered her with a grin.

"Welcome Mr. Jacobs. I also hope that you have a pleasant stay in our town, but I can't say that I am happy about the reason you are here," Jane commented to Simon.

"I understand Mrs. Taylor, but it's my job, and I try to do it to the best of my ability," answered Simon.

Jane nodded at him and gave him his room key. "Your room is up the stairs and to the right. "I hope you enjoy your stay with us. Breakfast is served starting at 7:00 AM in the dining room," Jane informed him.

Audrey Corbin came back down the stairs shortly before four o'clock to join Jane for tea. They went into the dining room, found a table in the corner where Audrey could observe the room and the people and ordered tea and biscuits.

"I was so impressed by what Albert told me about Rawlings that I wanted to see it firsthand. How did you and your husband happen to settle here?" Audrey asked Jane.

"My sister and brother-in-law heard about the town of Rawlings when we were living in Portland.

George and Marie were not excited about raising their family in Portland and the opportunities for the children to get into trouble were not as great here. George read about the hotel being for sale, investigated and decided to buy it sight unseen. Steven and I were married in Portland and decided to move here also. My mother was still alive so she came also, along with George and Marie's four children. Valerie their youngest daughter was born after they moved here," Jane explained to Audrey.

"That was quite a leap of faith that they took," Audrey stated.

"Yes it was, but George knew that it was the right place to raise his family. The people were so welcoming and kind and we all made good friends right away," explained Jane.

"This would make a great place to have a retirement home. I crave the quiet. Is there a lot of fishing around here?" Audrey asked Jane.

"People fish in the Snake River and there are small streams around the area that have some beautiful trout in them. "Why, do you fish?" asked Jane with a chuckle in her voice.

"As a matter of fact, yes I do! Albert and I love to get out and do some fishing. It is so relaxing. Albert gets out there on the banks of a river and forgets about all the stress of the job," said Audrey. "And we are alone. There is no secretary and no butler to bother us. We talk to each other very quietly when we are fishing. We are able to talk about our lives and the lives of our children without being interrupted."

Albert walked into the dining room followed by Thomas and Irene Campbell. Audrey had not seen Thomas since he was married and had not yet met Irene.

"Hello Audrey," Thomas said. "It is so good to see you. Welcome to Rawlings."

"Thank you Thomas. And you must be Irene. You are lovely, just as Albert said you were," Audrey said as she rose and shook Irene's hand.

Jane got up and gave Irene a big hug. "How are you doing, sweet girl?" she asked Irene.

"Just fine Aunt Jane," Irene said with a grin on her face. Jane turned to Audrey and explained that Irene was her niece. She was George and Marie's second daughter.

"You have a large family don't you," Audrey stated.

"Yes," Irene answered. "Mama and Papa had five children. Anna is the oldest and she lives in Lewiston. Then there's me. And then Charlotte. She is a nurse in Spokane. Freddie runs this hotel and Valerie is the baby. She just got married in April. She and Bill live on their farm just outside of town."

"My sister Susan and her husband Jeff own the JSJ Ranch just outside of town. They have one son, Jeffrey Jr. who is in his last year of school at Washington State in Pullman. When he finishes, he will come home and help Jeff on the ranch. Jeff Jr. is majoring in agriculture and will be a great asset to the ranch and to the community."

"Then there is our William. He is Anna's son, but he lives with us. He is the joy of our lives right now. Our twin boys are living back east, going to medical school. We do not see them very often. Their schedules do not give them much time to come way out here to visit," added Jane.

"My goodness! What a diverse family," Audrey declared.

"Until I hear a list of all of us, I don't realize how many of us there are," stated Steven.

Judge Corbin made short work of Otis Kingman's hearing. The evidence against him was overwhelming and he was sent back to Walla Walla State Penitentiary for being a convicted felon with a firearm and for pointing that firearm at the person of Fredrick Severs and destruction of property.

The whole town breathed a sigh of relief.

CHAPTER 11

Anna was lonely in Lewiston. She worked at the lounge and came home to an empty room in the boarding house. She did not have many friends and her relationship with her boss, Joe Archer was a little shaky.

Joe felt that she had been a little moody lately and had taken it out on some of the customers and they complained to him. He had talked to her about her attitude, but she didn't think she had done anything wrong.

Anna wanted her family but did not know how to approach them about coming to Rawlings for a visit. She decided to write to Irene and let her know what she had in mind. Since her parents were no longer living in Rawlings, she couldn't rely on them to intercede where the rest of her family was concerned.

Anna explained to Irene in the letter that she missed them, wanted to come for a visit to see them all and would not interfere at all with William. She explained that she knew in her heart that William was better off living with Jane and Steven than with her. She asked Irene if it would be okay if she came for a few days. She said that she knew she had a lot to make up for and wanted to start making amends. She told Irene that it would be best to write her back. It was hard for her to take personal phone calls at work.

Anna continued to work her schedule and waited for a letter from Irene. Joe was very cold and distant to her and she was uncomfortable around him. She was afraid he was going to fire her but knew that he had no one else to take her shift.

In the meantime, the citizens of Rawlings were getting ready to vote on the establishment of a city government and vote for a mayor. Steven Taylor, Earl Jansen, and Ray Clausen were the candidates for Mayor. All three had pretty much the same vision for Rawlings so it was a matter of who's vision they liked the best and who they thought would do the best job of conducting the business of the city.

Election day, November 13, 1906, was a cold but clear day and the registered voters showed up to vote at either the church or the hotel lobby depending on where they lived.

The two polling places were open from 8:00 AM to 3:00 PM. That gave everyone a chance to vote.

The Rev. John Simons, Dr. Blake Stephens and Jeff Jordan were all asked to count the votes. All ballots were verified to make sure that the person was registered, then were counted by the three men. The results of the election were announced the next morning.

Ray Clausen was elected Mayor of the city of Rawlings. He was very surprised at his election but was grateful for the show of confidence. Now it was time to get to work and form a city government. He had a lot to learn and a lot of decisions to make.

Ray's first job was to hire an assistant blacksmith. He was busy all of the time and needed help. He wired an ad to several newspapers advertising an opening for a blacksmith. He hoped that it would not be long before he had an answer and could hire someone. He was anxious to get on with the job of being mayor of Rawlings.

Irene received the letter from Anna and was stunned to hear from her. She did not open the letter immediately but waited to be with Thomas when she opened it.

"I am not sure why she would write to me unless it was to inquire about William," Irene mentioned to Thomas.

"Go ahead and open the letter, then we will know what she wants," said Thomas.

Irene opened the letter and read the first part of it. "She says she is lonely and wants to see her family. According to what she wrote, it sounds like she wants to make amends."

"I was under the assumption that she didn't think she did anything wrong," said Thomas. "How would you like to take a couple of days off of school and take the train to Lewiston and see her?" asked Thomas. "Maybe Fiona would take the class for a couple of days. We could go on a Thursday and come back on Sunday," explained Thomas.

"I think that would be a great idea. Since we do not know her intentions, I would rather not expose William to any of her antics at this time. He is settling in so nicely and doing very well in school. He has made some friends and spending some quality time with them. I would hate to interfere with that," explained Irene. "I will talk with Fiona and see if she would take the class for Thursday and Friday. Should we let Anna know we are coming or should we catch her off guard?" Irene asked Thomas.

"It would be the kind thing to do to let her know we are coming," Thomas answered.

After school on Monday, Irene went over to the hotel to see Jane. She wanted to show Anna's letter to her and ask her opinion and to let her know that she and Thomas were taking the train to Lewiston on Thursday.

"Everything is going along so well for William. I hope that Anna doesn't upset him. His emotional wellbeing is still a little fragile.

Anna was getting nervous about her letter to Irene. She had heard nothing from her and wasn't sure what her response would be. She wanted to get on the train and go to Rawlings, but was not sure whether she would be at all welcome, even to stay at the hotel.

She finally got a note from Irene saying that she and Thomas would be coming to Lewiston to see her. Irene had made a reservation at the Lewiston Hotel for Thursday evening November 22nd and they would leave to return to Rawlings on Sunday, the 25th.

"Joe, my sister, and brother-in-law are coming into town for a visit on Thursday. May I please have Friday the 23rd off to visit with them?" asked Anna when she went into work that evening.

"Do you think it will change your attitude to visit with your family?" Joe asked sarcastically. "You sure have been a little testy lately," he added.

"I miss my family and want to see them. At one time I thought that all I wanted was to be away from their control, but I realize now that I miss them. Sometimes, I even miss having William around. At least he was another human being to keep me company. Right now, there is no one besides you and the customers," Anna explained.

"Yes, you can have the night off, but you need to seriously change your attitude. You have offended some of our regular customers and that is not good for business," answered Joe.

"Thanks Joe. I will do better once I see my sister," Anna promised.

Irene was nervous as she and Thomas boarded the train to Lewiston on Thursday. She was not sure what Anna wanted and was apprehensive about the response to their visit. But she agreed with Thomas that it was better that they go to her instead of her coming to Rawlings.

"You know sweetheart, this will be my first trip to Lewiston," Irene said to Thomas as they settled into their seats on the train.

"Mine too," said Thomas. He had never had a cause to go there and Lewiston was not a big tourist attraction. Even though it was in beautiful country, it was not a big city like Portland or Seattle or even Boise.

Anna was very nervous as she was waiting for the train to arrive from Rawlings. She had to work

Thursday evening but would be off for Friday and Saturday and would go back to her regular shift on Sunday evening.

As Irene and Thomas stepped off of the train, they saw Anna waiting there for them. Irene walked up to her sister and tapped her on the shoulder saying, "Hello there Sister. You are looking good."

Anna whirled around startled at the tapping on her shoulder. She stopped herself before she said anything bad and gave Irene a brief hug. "Hello Irene. You are looking good also. Marriage agrees with you. Hello Thomas," Anna added.

"Hello Anna. It is good to see you again." Replied Thomas.

"I have booked you a room at the Lewiston Hotel. I have to work my regular shift this evening, but have tomorrow and Saturday off, so we can visit then. I have a lot to talk to you about," explained Anna.

The three of them walked to the hotel from the train station and Thomas checked them into their room.

"I have to go to work in about 30 minutes, so I will see you for breakfast in the morning. The dining room here has a decent breakfast. It's not as good as Papa's was, but it is passable," Anna explained to Irene. "I will meet you in the dining room at 8:30 AM if that is a good time for you."

"That will be fine with us. We will see you then. Have a good evening at work," said Irene.

"Thanks," answered Anna as she turned and walked into the lounge area to start her shift behind the bar.

Irene walked over to Thomas at the hotel desk. He was just finishing up the check-in process when he turned to her.

"That was awkward," commented Irene. "She talked like she had rehearsed for a long time what she was going to say."

"She probably did rehearse," commented Thomas. "I am sure she went over it several times in her head. She has a lot to atone for if that is what she has in mind for this visit. I really couldn't read her that well and I usually can read people. It is a skill that any lawyer should have."

Thomas and Irene settled their luggage into their room and decided to tour the town a bit. They found a small café where they ordered pasta with chicken for dinner and sat and did one of their favorite past-times, people-watching.

They also speculated on what Anna was going to say. They were truly afraid for William's well-being if she tried to get custody of him again.

"Let's not speculate on what she is going to say. We will deal with that when she tells us. Let's enjoy this evening. I appreciate having an evening alone with you where we will not be interrupted by anyone. I love you, Mrs. Campbell. Thank you for being my wife," whispered Thomas as he hugged her and kissed her.

"I love you too, my husband. You have given me my life," answered Irene.

Anna spent the evening doing her job and wondering how she was going to approach Irene and

Thomas tomorrow morning. She did not sleep very well that night. She was still trying to decide how she was going to tell Irene and Thomas how sorry she was about all of the trouble she caused about William. She still wanted to be accepted by her family but wanted them to know that she did feel remorse about her actions. She was afraid they would not believe her.

Thomas and Irene met Anna in the hotel dining room on Friday morning for breakfast. Anna had walked from her room at the boarding house to the hotel. She had a heavy coat and gloves on and by the time she got her coat off and hung up, the waiter had served her coffee. It was cold and windy outside and they were expecting a winter storm to come in over the weekend. Anna was grateful for the hot coffee to warm her up a bit.

"How late did you work last night Anna," asked Thomas.

"I was there until 2:00 AM. I worked my shift plus my bosses shift. I did that so that I could have this weekend off. My boss does not have anyone that is capable of working the late shift or is able to close down for the night," explained Anna.

"You must be tired today," stated Irene.

"No, I am okay. I often work the two shifts, especially when he wants some time off," stated Anna.

The three of them ordered their breakfasts and then Anna said, "I might as well get this conversation started. I want to apologize for my actions in the past. I have had a lot of time to do some soul searching in the past year and realize that I was totally out of control. I am not sure why I acted like I did. I do know that I resented the fact that I had William without my husband present. I was so upset with Will for lying to me about the time he would be away. He told me that he would only be gone for three months and would come back to Astoria and get me. I was convinced that he was telling me the truth until Papa talked to the shipping company dispatcher and he explained that they could be gone up to three years."

"Did Will know you were going to have a baby?" Irene asked.

"No! I did not know when he left that I was with child. It was about 2 weeks after he left that I suspected that I was pregnant. I was so angry that Will had left me more or less stranded in Astoria. I was living in a run-down boarding house room on the waterfront and found a job in a seedy bar also along the waterfront boardwalk," said Anna.

"Papa asked the Sorensons to come and get me and take me to Portland, but I did not want to go because I thought Will would be back to get me soon. They finally convinced me that by leaving a message at the shipping office, Will would be able to get in touch with me in Portland."

"I know that none of this excuses me for my later actions, but I want to give you the background of my pregnancy with Will. It was a very difficult pregnancy and birth. Even though Mama had given birth to all of you and I was around for the pregnancies, I didn't really pay any attention to her or her feelings. I was too interested in what I wanted and wasn't interested in Mama or her condition. All I could think about was how fat she was getting and the work it was going to take to care for a new baby. It only took Mama and Papa's attention away from me," continued Anna.

"Only recently, I began to feel terribly lonesome for my family. When Mama and Papa moved from Rawlings to Cannon Beach, I realized that they would probably not be back. Then I realized the rest of you probably wouldn't have much to do with me because of the way I have acted in the past. I want to make amends to all of you for my actions in the past. I know that it will take a long time for you to trust me, but I want to try," Anna said.

"We are concerned about William. None of us want his life disturbed or him to be in upheaval again. He is finally able to go to school and is making some friends. He has his dog and has a horse of his own at Jeff and Susan's ranch. He has more happy days than sad days now and none of us want that to change," exclaimed Thomas.

"We want his happy days to continue. I know that he is much better off with Steven and Jane. They love him and care for him like he should be," stated Irene firmly.

"Anna, it is going to be hard to convince the family that you mean what you are saying. I am leaning towards believing you right now, but I also know that you have, in the past, said things just to put yourself in a good light. May I suggest that you write a letter to the rest of the members of your family restating what you have said to Thomas and me here? You need to include Mama, Papa, Charlotte, Valerie, Freddie, Susan, and Jeff and of course Steven and Jane in that letter. But please do not include William. He is too young to understand what happened before he was born," said Irene with conviction. "You have hurt a lot of people and have a lot to atone for."

"I know that I have a lot of making up to do. Thomas, I am surprised that you will even talk to me after the way I treated you during the custody hearing," Anna reminded. "Slapping you in the face certainly didn't help my cause any."

"No, it didn't, but I think that is the least of your worries as far as the family is concerned. Your reaction to William's situation and how sincere you are in wanting to keep him with Steven and Jane is all important now. The family has to believe you are sincere in your desire for his wellbeing before they will consider bringing you back into the fold. The letter you write to them will have to be the best letter you have ever written if you want them to accept you again," said Thomas with a sincere voice.

After they had breakfast and talked for a while, Anna asked if they wanted to see some of the city of Lewiston. They were fairly close to the campus of the Lewis Clark Normal School. It was a very pretty campus and a pleasant place to walk. The weather was cold, but there was no sign of snow as yet and would make a nice walk after a meal.

They started walking around the campus and Anna explained that she was talking about possibly taking some classes. The school had courses in teaching, but also in cooking and homemaking. The also offered some courses in secretarial skills. She was not interested in becoming a teacher and cooking and homemaking did not interest her at all, but she thought that she might like to take come classes in secretarial skills, like typing, and shorthand. The thought of working regular hours and not having to deal with drunks all of the time appealed to her.

"Anna, I think that would be a great idea. It would be a relief to know that you were not working at night and have a better paying job. Thomas can tell you that there are lawyers who are always looking for skilled stenographers," Irene said.

"That's right. Skilled stenographers are hard to find, especially in smaller cities. It would take some specialized training to become a legal secretary, but you could do it if you had the desire and did well in your other classes. Irene is helping me now and it is very nice to have her around but she is not a secretary. She does type a little, but not as good as a stenographer would," Thomas said.

It was getting chilly outside and Thomas hired a hansom cab to take them back to the hotel. Anna decided to go on to her boarding house to start work on the all-important letter she had to write.

"You give us a call when you are ready for supper and we will pick you up. It is too cold for you to walk that far," Thomas commented. He asked the cab driver to take Anna home and he and Irene went into the hotel.

*C*HAPTER 12

Anna sat in her room thinking how she would start the letter to her family. She knew that she would have to write several different letters and wanted to get each one of them right. The letter to Steven and Jane would have to be totally different than the letter to Mama and Papa. Charlotte's letter and Freddie's letter would have to be different than Valerie's and Bill's. How to start????

She would start with Mama and Papa.

Dear Mama and Papa:

You are probably very surprised to get this letter from me. Thomas and Irene came to Lewiston to visit with me this weekend. I wrote them telling them that I missed the family and would like to come to Rawlings to see them. They both decided it was best if they came here. They were probably right. I do miss my family so much and know that I have acted very badly towards all of you, especially William.

I want you all to know that I have no claim on William and will not ever try to take him away from Steven and Jane. He belongs with them. I do not have the inclination or the skills to raise him. I am very sorry for the way I treated him. I was so wrapped up in myself and my wants that I did not think of him or anyone else for that matter.

I am not sure what happened to me long ago. I became so involved in what I wanted and didn't care about anyone else. I remember when I was young and you trying to break me from being a bully. I listened to you but I did not hear you. That was my problem.

I am truly sorry for what I have put you through. I hope that someday you can find it in your hearts to forgive me.

I love you with all my heart. Hopefully, I can see you again someday.

Love,
Anna

Anna read over the letter to her parents. She tried to be as sincere as she could and decided to send it as originally written.

Her next letter would be to Jeff and Susan. She wanted to apologize for her actions at Thomas and Irene's wedding.

The letters to Charlotte and Freddie would be apologizing for being so mean to them when they were small and ignoring them. She wanted them to know that they deserved better than that from a big sister. They deserved respect.

The letter to Steven and Jane would be the hardest. She wanted them to know that she was profoundly sorry for all of the terrible things she had said about them. She wanted them to know and believe that she had no claim on William. She did not want to interfere with their raising of William. She had to convince them that she had no desire to be involved in his life other than to be a member of the family.

> I understand that it will take time for you to believe me if you ever do. I want to make my life better and by doing that, I will need to convince you that I am truly sorry for all of the trouble I have caused you. You were so good to take William in when he needed someone.

Anna explained that she was taking stock of her life and trying to figure out and accept what went wrong years ago.

> I know that you will be skeptical of this letter and my intentions and I understand that. I want you to understand though, that I love my family and want to be a part of it.

> I am seriously thinking of signing up for some classes here at the Normal School. I feel that I would be good at secretarial skills and can learn to type and take shorthand with the goal of becoming a stenographer. I need a career other than being a bartender. I need to learn to like myself before other people can like me.

Anna wanted to make sure that her family understood her motives behind these letters. She hoped that they would be a start in bringing her back into the fold.

Anna showed the letter she wrote to her parents to Irene before she and Thomas left to return to Rawlings. Irene said that she thought the letter was good and would impress their parents.

Irene and Thomas hugged Anna before they boarded their train. They said that they would keep in touch and were relieved that the visit had gone so well. Both said that they were inclined to believe her motives.

Anna went back to her room and immediately decided to go to the college the next morning and investigate the possibility of signing up for classes starting in January. She wasn't sure how classes would work with her work schedule and need for sleep, but she was determined to make it work and build a better life and career for herself.

Anna signed up for two classes to begin with. She was able to afford the tuition because she had saved a lot of her pay since she had given up custody of William. She had a class in beginning typing and beginning shorthand. Her schedule did not interfere with her work schedule at the hotel. She had also decided not to say anything to Joe about her decision. She was afraid he would try to talk her out of going to school.

Christmas 1906 was a very busy time in Rawlings. The weather was cold, but it did not snow and ice over like it could have. The family was able to spend Christmas eve together at the hotel. They all went to church and then had a huge supper in the dining room of the hotel.

Christmas day was spent with Susan and Jeff at the ranch. Jeff Jr. was home as well as Charlotte. George and Marie were missed, but everyone was able to talk to them on the telephone on Christmas day. Anna was the only member of the family who was not contacted on Christmas day. Thomas and Irene talked to her briefly on Christmas eve, but no one else wanted to talk to her yet. They all received their letters but were not sure whether to believe what she wrote.

Steven and Jane both talked to their boys on Christmas day, but they were so far away and were not able to make the long trip home for such a short visit. They only had one more year of medical school, then would be able to come home for a visit before they returned for an internship in their chosen fields of medicine.

Bill and Valerie announced on Christmas day that they were going to have a baby in June 1907. The whole family was very excited about the news.

The couple had spent Christmas eve with Clyde and Virginia and the rest of the Kingman family and made the announcement to them. They were all looking forward to another baby to bring the family together.

William had a great Christmas. He was getting taller all of the time and received a lot of new clothes. Patch also received his fair share of balls, ropes, bones, and special treats. Patch was an important part of the family and received a gift from almost everyone, including the ranch hands.

"Thank you for a great Christmas," William said. "I really enjoyed myself and it was good to talk to Grandma and Grandpa. They sound like they are having a good time in Cannon Beach."

"Did you hear from your Mother, William?" asked Susan.

"No. I didn't expect to. We never celebrated Christmas when I was living with her. She always worked on Christmas day," answered William.

Susan thought to herself, "her loss!"

The year 1907 came in with a blast of cold, icy weather that kept most of the citizens of Rawlings inside or very close to their fires. Because of the weather, most of the students living on farms and ranches in the outlying areas did not get to school. They were busy taking care of the livestock and making sure that they were safe from the weather and predators. Work on the ranches and farms did not stop because of the weather.

The trains still stopped in Rawlings, with passengers making their way to the hotel for meals and one-night stays until the train left the next day. Freddie was continually busy and loved taking care of the guests. Jim Barnes, the cook at the hotel diner was busy creating new menus using the food that was available.

Steven was still doing the ordering for most of the needs of the dining room and the hotel and Jim was always adding to the list of ingredients when he wanted to create new and different dishes for the guests.

The Palouse and Nez Perce Indians continued to provide wild game to the hotel. In turn, they were given fruits and vegetables shipped in via train that they did not have access to otherwise.

From the time Freddie was a small child, he loved to visit the Indian villages with his father and Uncle Jeff and the Indians considered him a member of their tribe. He always welcomed his friends to the hotel, even though it shocked some of the guests. Many of the guests were from the east and were not used to seeing Indians in the cities.

The city of Rawlings was peaceful during the first half of 1907. Bill and Valerie Kingman had a baby girl in May 1907. They named her Virginia Marie Kingman and called her Ginny. Her grandma Virginia was thrilled to have her first grandchild. She and Clyde spent as much time with the baby as they could but tried not to interfere with the daily routine that Bill and Valerie had set.

William turned 12 years old in June and was excited to spend some time on the ranch with Uncle Jeff and Aunt Susan. He was still too young to ride the range with the cowboys, but there were some jobs that he could do and he was excited to spend time with Seth and Daniel Kingman. They were his idols as far as the cowboys were concerned. Both Seth and Daniel were very patient with William and were very willing to let him tag along while they worked. William learned a lot by just watching them, but he did ask a lot of questions. They always answered him. Both of them remembered when they first moved out to the ranch and how good it was to have someone who took an interest in them.

Blake Stephens, the town doctor, was thinking seriously about getting a motor car. The electric motorcar was introduced into both Walla Walla and Spokane in 1905. The roads between the two towns were not good for motor car travel, but the roads in the city of Rawlings and its surrounding area were not bad. They were flat but rutted from the wagon wheels. They would have to be graded to make a road trip comfortable. Blake wanted the car for travel to and from farms and ranches when he had house calls. He felt it would be easier than having to hook the horse to the buggy each time he had to make a call.

"Fiona, I am going to check out the possibility of getting a motor car," Blake mentioned to his wife.

"Why would you want a motor car," she asked.

"I think it would be more efficient than having to saddle the horse, or hook a horse to the buggy," Blake answered. "I won't do anything yet. I just want to check it out. Jeff was also talking about a motor car, but he thinks there will be an alternative fuel source developed soon and he wants to wait for that.

His purpose would be to have a truck that could haul hay to the cattle. For the time being, the horse and buggy work fine.

"I have seen pictures of those motor cars. It seems to me that a person would get awfully dirty riding one in the summer months and awfully cold in the winter months. There should be some way of enclosing them to protect the passengers," Fionna commented.

"Maybe someday," Blake thought out loud.

The year 1907 was turning out to be a profitable year for Rawlings. Bill and Valerie Kingman had a baby and were doing well on their farm. The hotel and the dining room were continuing to be profitable for Freddie. James Kingman was learning to run the general store and doing a fine job of keeping it profitable. Steven was still the postmaster and his accounting business was growing. The town had a lawyer in residence with Thomas Cambell moving to Rawlings. The citizens of Rawlings were happy with the way the new government was operating and appreciated the improvements that were made.

There were a few minor problems in setting up the city government. There were telephone wires strung in the wrong places and some of the roads were not plowed when they were supposed to be, but Sam Clausen handled all of the complaints with quiet efficiency. He was a very good choice for mayor.

William spent part of the summer at the JSJ Ranch learning how to be a cowboy. He had his own horse stabled there and was always eager to ride with the ranch hands. He did not go on any of the long rides but did some rounding up of cattle close to the main compound. He loved being able to ride his horse and his fondest dream was to be a cowboy. He wanted to go on the longer rides when the hands would stay in the line shacks and be out for several days at a time, but Jeff thought he was still too young for that and he was not as skilled a rider yet to take on a full roundup.

It seemed that the year went by very quickly and soon it was the holiday season again. This fall and winter, the weather was not cooperating the way it had in past years and it was difficult for families to get together. Jim Barnes cooked his usual Christmas dinner at the hotel, but the weather kept a lot of people from eating there. A few passengers came in on the train and had to stay over because of some trouble down the line, but it was not the usual Christmas celebration at the hotel.

The Indians came into town with their usual gift of wild game and were given a lot of the leftover Christmas dinner in return. This year they gifted Freddie a beautiful elk skin jacket made by the women of the tribe. Freddie cherished that jacket and wore it often in the cold and inclement weather. He wore it like a badge of honor and it became one of his prized possessions.

Anna was busy all of the time now. She loved school. She was able to purchase a used typewriting machine and practiced her typing skills as much as she could. Shorthand was a little more difficult, but she worked hard in class and tried to study and practice away from class. One evening she even tried to take drink orders with shorthand but decided that wasn't such a good idea when she got the orders mixed up. Fortunately, Joe was not there to see it. He still didn't know that she was going to school.

Anna made sure that she was on time to work every day. She was afraid to let Joe know that she was going to school. She was afraid he would fire her and then she would not be able to continue with school.

Besides taking typing and shorthand, Anna was taking a class in general office skills. There was a skill to learning to file papers properly, on how to take phone messages and how to greet clients either over the phone or in person. Her ability to do all of this would make a big difference in whether she would be able to get and keep a job as a stenographer.

One of Anna's greatest pleasures was being able to get out of her room, go to school and meet other people with the same interests as she had. She was in a class of women who really wanted to learn their craft. She still had to spend her evenings serving drinks to men, but she had a much better feeling about herself. And she was making friends for the first time and not feeling any jealousy or animosity towards them for having anything more or less than she had.

Even though Anna was older than most of the girls in her classes, she did not look it and did not tell them that she was a bartender in the evening. She wanted to keep her two lives separate.

Thomas and Irene continued to correspond with Anna and were pleased with what she told them about school. They were glad she was trying to make a better life for herself although not 100 percent sure that she could do it. "At least she's trying," Irene commented to Thomas one evening while speaking about her.

Aside from the initial letters that Anna had written to the rest of her family, she had not written to any of them again. Aside from her parents, the only return letter she had received was from Charlotte saying that she really, at this time, had no desire to see Anna. She was too busy with her career and did not live close enough to visit. She wished her well in her endeavors. She just signed it "Charlotte."

Anna had hoped for more of a response from her family but was not surprised when she did not hear from any more of them. Her parents had, of course, contacted her. Even though she had hurt them by her actions and comments, they still loved her dearly and did not want to lose contact with her. They were excited about her decision to go to school and work towards a better career.

Anna did not have a phone in her room at the boarding house and had to use the house phone when she wanted to make or receive a call. Her boss, Joe had called her one day wanting her to come in to work early. Her landlady answered the phone and told Joe that she was not there, she was in school. He was surprised about the school comment but did not say anything. He asked the landlady to give her a message that he needed her to come in to work two hours early.

When Anna received the message, she had only about a half hour to get to work. When she went in about 10 minutes late, Joe confronted her with a question about her going to school.

"What are you going to school for?" he asked forcefully.

Anna could tell he was angry and was afraid that he would fire her on the spot. "I am taking a secretarial course at the Normal School," she quietly told him.

"Why?" he demanded.

Anna was getting mad and answered him. "Because I do not want to be a bartender for the rest of my life. I want a job that has normal hours and that I can be proud of."

"Are you going to quit this job?" Joe asked.

"Not until I finish school and get a job as a stenographer," answered Anna. "I would like to work for you until then. I cannot afford to continue with school unless I have a job."

"Get to work then. We will discuss this later," said Joe.

Anna worked her shift that evening with the fear that she would not have her job when her shift was over. She knew Joe was angry with her for not telling him about her classes, but it was her personal decision and she didn't think it was his business at the time.

When Anna's shift was over, Joe asked her into his office. She was tired and still had some homework to do for tomorrow's shorthand class.

"Anna, tell me what your intentions are," said Joe.

"I was afraid to say anything to you for fear you would fire me and I need this job to continue to go to school. I have been very grateful for this job, but honestly do not want to be a bartender for the rest of my life. I have really made a mess of my relationship with my family and miss them. I would like to better myself and get some sort of relationship back with them," explained Anna.

"What about your son?" asked Joe.

"I explained to my sister that I have no desire to disturb his life with Steven and Jane. I am not equipped to take care of him or be a mother to him. I was truly serious when I gave up custody of him," said Anna.

"Will you try to get a job as a secretary here in Lewiston?" asked Joe.

"I don't know. I would like to either go back to Rawlings or maybe go to the Oregon beach where my parents are," answered Anna. "I am not sure whether Rawlings has any place for me to work as a stenographer. I am not sure what I am going to do or where I am going to go, I just know that I need to do something different than what I am doing now.

"I hate to see you leave this job, but I do understand your need to have a better life. You have this job until you are ready for something else. Please just give me some notice before you leave. It is going to be hard for me to find someone to replace you," Joe explained.

Chapter 13

Anna completed her classes at Lewis Clark Normal School in December of 1907. She did an outstanding job and was an honor student in her graduating class. She had not planned on going through the graduation ceremony but was persuaded by Joe to participate. Even though he did not want to lose her as an employee, he was very proud of her for taking the initiative to complete her classes.

Anna wrote to Irene to let her know that she had graduated and was a qualified stenographer. She also asked if Irene thought it would be possible for her to visit Rawlings without causing too much disturbance among the family. She wanted to see her family in person to try to explain and apologize for her actions.

When Irene received Anna's letter, she was put in the difficult position of asking all of the family if they would object if Anna came for a visit. Irene was not happy being put into this position, but figured since she was the next oldest child, it was her responsibility.

Because of the weather, it was decided that it would be best if Anna waited until Springtime to visit the family.

Anna accepted the decision to wait and started looking for a stenographer job in Lewiston. There were none to be found. It was the wrong time to be looking for work. In the meantime, she still had her job in the lounge at the Lewiston Hotel to fall back on. She would job search in the mornings and work at the lounge from three until closing. It was usually about 2:00 AM when she was able to get out of there. She was so tired when she got home from work that she just fell into bed.

Steven and Jane had never lied to William about the situation with his mother. He knew what she was and how she had treated her family. Since there was talk about her coming back into town in the spring, Steven decided that it was time to sit down with William and explain the situation.

"William, your mother has written to the family about coming back to Rawlings for a while. She has written to all of the family to apologize for her actions in the past and wants to see all of us. She says she is very sorry that she hurt us. We all are concerned about you and your feelings. Your mother says that she does not want to disrupt your life now and does not want custody back. She accepts the fact that she is not capable of taking care of you or seeing to your needs. I want to know how you feel about seeing her again," explained Steven.

"I am not sure. I want to see her but I am afraid. She might want me to go back to Lewiston with her. I do not want to leave Rawlings," answered William.

"I do not think that will be a problem," said Steven.

William and Steven were out for a short walk to the general store. William stopped outside the store and looked into the window, not really seeing what was there, but thinking about all of the lonely times with his mother and how many times he had craved her attention. He turned around and started walking back home. He had tears in his eyes and did not want anyone to see him crying.

"I do not want to see her if she is going to say mean things to me again. I know that Uncle Thomas will make sure that I do not have to live with her again. He promised me when I came to live with you, but I am afraid she will make me cry in front of everyone," William answered.

"You know William, I can make sure that you are at the ranch with Seth and Daniel when she arrives if that would make you feel better. We can have a chance to see her and talk to her before she sees and talks to you," commented Steven with concern in his voice. "Everyone in the family wants you to be comfortable and feel safe."

"Thank you Uncle Steven. That would be good to be with Seth and Daniel. Maybe they would let me ride out with them?" questioned William.

"We'll see! I still don't know when she will be coming. It will most likely be on a weekend. She just graduated from a secretarial course at the college in Lewiston and will be looking for a different job. She does not want to be a bartender anymore," said Steven.

William turned around and headed back for the store after he dried the tears from his face. As he and Steven were entering the store, Dr. Stephens was coming in also.

"Hello you two!" Dr. Stephens said. "Out to buy something?"

"No, just walking and looking. Maybe we'll get some candy," answered Steven.

William walked away to look at some books that Clyde had just put out on the shelf. Dr. Stephens asked Steven in a low voice, "Anything wrong?"

"Not really. His mother wants to come to town to visit the family and he is worried about having to return to her care. We have all assured him that the custody is permanent and she would have to petition the court again if she wanted him back. She assures us all that she does not. She misses being a part of the family and has apologized to all of us for her actions. Needless to say, we are a little skeptical," explained Steven.

"I don't blame you after all of her antics in the past," said the doctor.

William was looking at the books and talking to James about them when Steven came up behind him to see what book he was interested in. It was a book about motorcars and how they worked. He was also interested in the new invention, so asked William if he would like to have that book.

"Oh, yes!" answered William. "Someday when I am old enough, I am going to have one of these and drive it to Oregon to see Grandma and Grandpa."

Steven chuckled at him as he took the book up to the counter to pay for it. The doctor and Clyde were deep in a discussion about cars and how they would be fueled. Gasoline was being used as a fuel for motor vehicles on the east coast and it would be very soon that they would be able to get barrels of gasoline shipped in by rail car.

"Clyde, in order to have the gasoline cars, the town needs a place to fill them with fuel and the general store is the logical place to do that. An underground tank would have to be installed and a pump put in above it in order to fill the cars," explained Dr. Stephens.

"Seems to me it would be expensive," commented Clyde.

"The initial outlay of money would be large, but I know that you would recoup that money very quickly with the number of people who would need fuel for their cars. It will not be long before the road is improved between Dayton and Colfax and you know very well that road comes directly through Rawlings," said the doctor.

"Also, I have heard that a lot of the ranchers in the area are interested in gasoline trucks for use on their places. They would have to buy the fuel through you. You would be the only distributor in the area authorized to purchase and sell gasoline," stated Dr. Stephens.

Clyde brought his head up at that statement. "That is something to think about. Let me talk to Virginia and James about this idea and I will let you know what we decide. James is included now in all of the major decisions where the store is concerned. He will run it someday and has to be aware of what is to come."

"Sounds good, Clyde. Have a great day!" the doctor said as he was leaving the store. "Goodbye William. Goodbye Steven," he added as he walked out.

The main topic of conversation around town was the possibility of installing a gasoline pump in front of the general store. Mayor Sam even brought it up in the next city council meeting.

"There would have to be some strict city regulations in force to guard against fire and explosion. Gasoline is very volatile and you have to be extremely careful around it," explained Sam.

Thomas Campbell added, "If we have cars on the roads, we will have to maintain the roads. The logical place we can get the money to maintain the roads is to add a tax to each gallon of gasoline sold. It would be a city tax and used strictly for maintenance of the roads."

Jeff Jordan added, "If we have farm vehicles and need to have gasoline delivered to our farms, how is it transported?"

"There are questions that will have to be worked out. No one has a car yet and we, as yet, do not have the need for a gasoline pump. Let's all think about the possibility though and come up with ideas and needs that the town will have," added Sam. "I appreciate you all coming to this meeting today. This is going to be an important addition to our town and we want to do it right the first time and not have to make any corrections to laws or statutes later."

Life continued in Rawlings with much talk about transportation and the way people got from one place to another. There were some of the older cowboys who thought that the horse and buggy would never be replaced. Nothing could surpass the stamina of a good horse. Then there were others who said the motorized vehicle was the only way to go.

Anna made plans to visit Rawlings in the late part of June 1908. Joe had given her a week off of work so she would have plenty of time to visit and not have to rush back to Lewiston.

She was anxious and a little scared when she boarded the train for Rawlings. Irene and Thomas were the only ones who knew the exact date she was coming. She would stay at their house in the spare bedroom. Irene felt the hotel was a little too public.

"I think we could host the family here, Thomas," mentioned Irene. "If there are other diners in the restaurant, we do not want all of the family secrets out in public."

"That would be fine dear, if you think that you can handle it," answered Thomas.

"I think I can," said Irene.

When Anna's train arrived, Thomas was there to pick her up in the buggy. They greeted each other and he took her directly to his home. Anna was impressed with the house. It was a small light blue house with a white fence round the yard. Irene had planted bright flowers in boxes on the porch. It was very pretty.

Irene greeted Anna at the door with a brief hug and showed her to the spare bedroom so she could freshen up before supper.

Supper that evening was a simple meat loaf with vegetables. All three of them talked about what would happen the next day at the noon dinner that was being planned. Irene explained that the family would meet there and have a potluck type meal together.

"I feel that being here instead of the hotel would allow you more privacy to say what you want to each member of the family. And, by the way, William will not be here. He is spending the weekend with some friends and does not know you are in town," Thomas said with relief.

"That's good. I have not quite come to terms with speaking to him as yet. I am not sure how to approach him. I do not want to scare him and I do not want to hurt him. I know I was very cruel to him and I am earnestly sorry for my behavior," Anna explained regretfully.

Thomas said, "Just tell him that, Anna. He is old enough and smart enough to understand."

"That is easier said than done Thomas," Anna said. "I have gone over and over in my mind what I would say to him. You know, I cannot remember giving birth to him. I have blocked all of that out of my memory. I can't even remember what his father looked like. I have stood before a mirror and tried to practice speaking to William, but nothing comes out. I don't even know what he looks like."

"You have a lot of repair work to be done Anna. Let's start with the family and see what happens there. Your relationship with William will eventually sort itself out," said Thomas.

The first to arrive at Thomas and Irene's home on Saturday were Valerie and Bill. They thought it was a good idea to leave Ginny with her Grandma Virginia for the afternoon. It would cause less stress and distraction. The next to arrive were Susan and Jeff. Susan was very cautious as she walked in. She was not sure how she would be received by Anna. Even with Jeff beside her, she was nervous.

Jane and Steven were the next to arrive. They were both nervous about seeing Anna. They had not seen each other since the court gave them custody of William. They were both afraid that Anna would want him back and they did not want that to happen. They knew that William did not want that either.

Charlotte came into town from Spokane especially for this meeting today. She was staying at the hotel and came with Freddie. Freddie was the only one in the family who did not have any reason to be angry with Anna. She pretty much ignored him for most of his life and that was fine with him.

Both Susan and Jane greeted Anna coldly. They were not sure what was going to be said or how they would react to her words. They were thinking about their sister Marie and about the difficulties that she had in raising Anna.

Dinner was ready by the time Charlotte and Freddie arrived and everyone sat down to eat. It was crowded, but Thomas managed to find chairs for everyone to sit around the table. Anna was sitting between Thomas and Irene. A prayer was said and the food was passed around the table. The men loaded up their plates, the ladies took very little and Anna took almost nothing. They were all apprehensive about what would be said and what their feelings would be. None of them wanted to get angry or upset. They all wanted this meeting to go well and all of them wanted William to be safe and happy and they felt that a lot of what Anna wanted to talk about had to do with William.

"Thank you all for coming today. Anna requested this visit so that she could start the process of healing some wounds that she caused and to make amends for the wrongs that she did. So, Anna, the floor is yours!" Thomas said as he sat down.

"Now that this time is here, I do not know where to start," Anna mumbled. "I have gone over this in my mind so many times and wondered how I could possibly make amends for all of the hurt that I have caused every one of you. I don't know if you will believe me or not, but I am truly sorry for the trouble I have caused. From the time I was very small, I wanted to be the best and have the best of everything. I resented Mama and Papa for having more children because that took the attention away from me. I am not sure why I was that way. I made trouble in school by bullying some of the people in the class. That, I know now, was uncalled for. I resented the fact that a new baby was coming into the family because it would take away attention from me. Aunt Susan, I can't tell you how sorry I am for the comments that I made to you when you announced that you were pregnant with Jeffrey. Charlotte, Irene, Freddie, and Valerie, I caused you so much grief in your childhoods, I cannot imagine it. I was selfish and arrogant and I am so sorry."

"What caused the turnaround Anna?" Jeff asked.

"I am not really sure. It was gradual I suppose. After William was gone, I only had myself to look out for. At first it was such a relief not having to be responsible for anyone else. I admit, I was not a good mother. I was shocked when I discovered I was pregnant. When I found out Will was dead, that was another shock. Then I found out that he lied to me, that seemed to pull the trigger. I pretty much gave up on being a parent. I really could not imagine what would happen to my life. When Mama and Papa brought us back here, they pretty much made me take care of William. I managed to take care of him physically, but emotionally I was a wreck. I do regret not taking better care of him, but I also do not regret giving custody of him to Steven and Jane. I was against it at first, but once I got back to Lewiston and realized I did not have another person to be responsible for, it was a relief."

"How do we know that you will not revert to your old ways?" asked Jane.

"You don't! All I can say is that I feel so much better about myself. I finished school and have a certificate to show that I am a qualified stenographer and secretary. By doing that, I have gained a lot of self-confidence and know that I am qualified to do a good job at my chosen profession. I am a good bartender, but that is not what I want to do for the rest of my life. I want a job that will possibly give me some respect from others. Bartending does not do that. I want a job where I can make friends with other people who have the same interests that I have. And I want to start reading books."

"That is hard to believe," Irene commented. "You always resented me having my nose in a book all of the time and ignoring you."

"I know, and I am very sorry. Since taking this course at Normal School, I realize that there is a whole world out there to explore. When I ran away from home, I thought that I would explore it in person, but now I realize that I can learn what I want by reading it in books," Anna mentioned.

"Irene, I am sorry that I spoiled the end of your wedding. You looked beautiful," Anna added.

"It was a lovely wedding. Anna, have you had any desire to get married again?" Susan asked.

"Heavens no! That is not even in my distant thoughts. I do know my limitations now and I know that I cannot live with anyone else. It would be a disaster for both of us," answered Anna.

Everyone at the table chuckled at that. Freddie, Charlotte, and Valerie had not said anything at all about Anna being there. All three had listened intently to what Anna had said but made no comment. None of them had much contact with Anna while growing up. Charlotte probably had the most contact, but she was so involved with Freddie, that she did not pay attention to what Anna said or did. Freddie did not have much contact with Anna at all. She ignored his presence and he ignored hers. He was happiest being with Uncle Jeff at the ranch, or with his papa when they went to the Indian villages.

Valerie did not really know Anna at all. She was very young and Anna had resented her being in the family. She was extremely angry at her Mama for having another baby, so she ignored Valerie completely. She would not acknowledge the existence of Valerie at all.

"Why didn't you like me?" Valerie finally asked.

"I resented Mama having another baby. Again, it would take away any attention that she would give to me. I am truly sorry that I did not get to know you. You are a lovely young lady, wife, and now I understand a mother. I am sorry that I can only call you my sister and not my friend. Maybe someday," Anna mused.

"Maybe we can try someday," answered Valerie.

Everyone finished their meal, put the dishes in the kitchen and were ready to leave. Anna was a little disappointed in the response that she received from everyone but realized that it would take some time for them to digest all that she had said.

*C*HAPTER 14

Susan and Jeff were very quiet on the way home. Both of them were trying to make sense of what Anna had said. They were trying to figure out if she really had changed or if it was an act she was putting on and if so, for what reason.

"I suppose we will have to be around her for a while to know if she is serious about making amends to the family. I am wondering how she will react to William now. I don't even know if he wants to see her," Susan said with apprehension in her voice.

"Would you like to invite her to dinner while she is in town?" asked Jeff.

"I was thinking that we probably should," answered Susan. "I think that Steven and Jane are afraid to ask about William. Even though Anna says that she does not want William back, I think Steven feels that if she sees him and sees what he is capable of now, she will try to get him back."

"He is a totally different boy now. Being able to read and do his arithmetic makes a difference. He is capable of so much more now." Jeff added.

Valerie and Bill went to the store to pick up Ginny. Virginia and Clyde and James still lived in the apartment above the store. It was the perfect size for them and both Clyde and James were close to work. Valerie had a hard time being away from Ginny for a very long time. She knew that she was perfectly okay with her grandma. Clyde would run upstairs once in a while to see how Ginny was. He had never been around babies before and they fascinated him.

Charlotte and Freddie left the dinner party wondering why they were really there. They had no problem with Anna. When they were small children, Anna ignored them. They did not get into fights with her or have any problems with her behavior. Charlotte remembered when they had to change bedrooms and Charlotte was the one to cause the problems.

Steven and Jane were not sure what to expect from Anna. They were terrified that she would try to take William back. They loved William dearly and did not want to lose him. Thomas said earlier that it would be a fight for her to get him back. It would really depend on how William felt.

William was having a great time at the ranch with Daniel and Seth. They took him out on the range with them looking for strays. It was a fairly easy job and wasn't a dangerous one in the good weather. William knew his mother was in town and was very nervous about seeing her. Uncle Steven had said that he did not have to see her if he did not want to, but William was not sure if his mother would insist or not. He was much happier being with Seth and Daniel.

When William got back to the ranch house in the late afternoon, he saw that Susan and Jeff were home. He was apprehensive but curious about what had happened at the dinner. He went into the house and directly to his room to wash up before he saw them. He didn't know if his mother was there or not.

He went down stairs and into the study to see Susan and Jeff. They were sitting before a fire talking about the dinner.

"Hi William! Come in and sit with us. How was your day?" asked Jeff.

"It was great! Daniel and Seth took me out on the range looking for strays. We found two yearlings, but nothing else. We did ride by the grist mill. It is too bad that it is not working," William answered.

"I wish I could have made a go of it too, but after Jesse left, I could not find anyone who would run it. I have to decide what we are going to do with the mill now, but I have been putting it off," replied Jeff.

"How was dinner at Aunt Irene's and Uncle Thomas' house?" asked William tentatively.

"Your mother was there, along with the rest of the family. She talked quite a lot about what had happened in her childhood and what her feelings were towards all of us. She said that she resented all of her sisters and her brother because they took her parents attention away from her. She admitted that she was jealous of all of us for what we had and for the attention that we got from other members of the family," explained Susan.

"She talked at length about you and her attempt at raising you. Your mother does admit that she did a terrible job of taking care of you. She resented the fact that she was pregnant with you without your father there to help her. She also finally realized that he had lied to her and was not going to be back in Astoria in 3 months. The shipping office told her that it could be more like 3 years if they ever made port in Astoria again. She couldn't believe that he had lied to her and she realized that she had been used," Jeff said.

"Does she want me to come back to Lewiston and live with her now?" mumbled William.

"No William. You are not to worry about that. She admitted that she was not capable of taking care of another person. Your mother has gone to school and received a certificate as a qualified stenographer and secretary. She is going to be looking for a job in that field. She says that she does not want to be a bartender for the rest of her life. She admits that she needs to work on healing herself. She says that she will never marry again, that she is not capable of living with another person," Susan answered William. She got up out of her chair and went to him and gave him a big hug. "Don't worry. You are in Rawlings for as long as you want to be and your Aunt Jane and Uncle Steven are your guardians. We all love you and are very glad you are a member of this family."

"Will I have to see her?" William asked.

"Only if you want to!" answered Jeff. "I think she would like to see you and explain her feelings to you. We are going to ask her here to dinner this week.

If you would like, you can be here. That way, we will be right here with you when you talk to her."

"I would like that," William said quietly. "I think I will go up to my room for a while. I have a book I would like to read. Thank you very much. I love you too!"

When William left the study, both Susan and Jeff looked at each other in astonishment. That was the first time either of them had heard William say he loved anyone. Both of them had tears rolling down their faces.

Anna was relieved that the dinner was over. She had said what she wanted to say and now she figured the rest was up to them. She just hoped that her family would believe that she was sincere in her desires to make amends to all of them. Right now, seeing William was her biggest worry. She was not sure how she would feel about seeing him or how he would feel about seeing her. She had been so terrible to him and had ignored him for so long, he must resent her terribly.

There was a knock on her bedroom door. "Anna, may I come in?" asked Irene.

"Yes, come on in," answered Anna.

"Susan just called and asked if you would come to the ranch on Wednesday for dinner. William will be there if you want to see and talk to him," Irene explained.

"Oh dear! I was just thinking about seeing him again. I guess it would be best if I was not alone. Is he living at the ranch now?" Anna asked.

"No, he is still living with Steven and Jane. That is his home and I think he feels safest there. And of course, during the school year, it is closer and he does love school. He spends time with his friends at the ranch on weekends and holidays. Anna, William is a very good student and a very good boy. He has learned so quickly in school and is working up to his grade level. He is intelligent and curious about everything. So, despite his early upbringing, he is doing extremely well. I would ask that you use care in talking to him. He is still very sensitive about his feelings toward you and has not sorted it all out yet," asked Irene with some authority in her voice.

"I will be careful," said Anna quietly.

Anna prepared very carefully for the dinner at Susan and Jeff's. Jeff had said he would send one of the hands in to get her in the buggy, so she would not have to get there on her own.

Jeff greeted her at the door and escorted her into the study. Anna had not been to their home and was very impressed with the place. The study was very cozy room with books lining the walls, a large, beautiful fireplace and a beautiful oak desk dominating one side of the room. William was standing by the fireplace as she entered. My how he had grown. He was tall and looked exactly like his father. Anna was shocked at the resemblance. It had been so long since she had thought about Will and how he looked. She just looked at William and couldn't say anything for a few seconds.

"You look exactly like your father!" exclaimed Anna.

"I sure hope I don't act like him!" William answered sarcastically.

"William, that was uncalled for," admonished Jeff.

"I'm sorry." William mumbled.

"Dinner is ready in the dining room," Susan said as she walked into the study. "Hello Anna. Welcome to our home."

"Thank you. It is very nice of you to invite me. You have a beautiful home.

They all followed Susan into the dining room. She had chosen to use the dishes and tableware that her father-in-law had given her and the table looked beautiful. Cora, the housekeeper/cook had fixed a beautiful roast for dinner. The ranch hands were lucky today. Joe, Cora's husband was the cook in the bunkhouse and had fixed pretty much the same dinner, but not with all the fancies added.

William sat down on the opposite side of the table from Anna. He was nervous about seeing her and talking to her and was sorry about the comment he made about his father. Uncle Jeff was right. It was uncalled for. He knew nothing about his father. His mother had never said a word about him. The only information he knew was what other people had said.

"You have grown very tall William. You will be tall like your father was," commented Anna.

"Do you have a picture of him?" asked William.

"Yes, I do, but it is a very old one. He was just a boy. It was in his steamer trunk that was sent to me after he died," Anna said to William. "I will send it to you if you would like it."

"Maybe someday," William mumbled as he ate a bite of his meal.

The four of them continued to eat their meal. Jeff occasionally asked a question about Lewiston and the surrounding area, which Anna answered politely.

"Anna, tell us about school. What made you decide to take classes at the Normal School?" asked Susan.

Anna perked up. This was a subject she could comfortably talk about. "Bartending is a very hard life and I did not want to be a bartender for the rest of my career. I inquired at the school about classes that I could take, not to get a degree in particular, but to be able to get a certificate to show that I was qualified to do the job. I knew for sure I did not want to be a teacher. The education field is the biggest department at the school. Nor did I want to be a homemaker. That is another large department. About the only thing left besides nursing, which they do not teach, was stenography. Working in an office appealed to me. I would still meet people, but on a more professional basis. So, I got all of the information I could and took several months to decide if that was what I wanted to do. After thinking about it for a time, I decided it was a career that I would enjoy and could do with some expertise if I really applied myself to it."

"Will you stay in Lewiston?" Jeff asked.

"I don't know. I would like to get away from there. I am afraid that some of the people in town will always think of me as a bartender. I worked in a very popular place and met a lot of the prominent people in town," Anna answered.

"I am thinking about going to visit Mama and Papa. I need to talk to both of them and apologize to both of them for my actions. I was a horrible daughter to them. I would also like to see the ocean. Papa kind of instilled that desire in all of us. I can remember him sitting in the evening talking about the Pacific Ocean and Lewis and Clark boiling sea water to get the salt to preserve their meat for the winter. I would like to experience the feeling he had the first time he saw it. He writes about the huge rock near where they live and about the way the waves crash to the shoreline in a storm. That fascinates me!" exclaimed Anna. "I was in Astoria, but never had a chance to see the actual ocean. I only had time to see the mouth of the river and the docks where the ships came in."

"William, would you mind if we talked for a bit? I have some things I would like to say to you," Anna asked.

"Okay. Can Uncle Jeff and Aunt Susan be there too?" William asked.

"Certainly! I want you to be comfortable," answered Anna.

"Let's move into the study," said Jeff.

They moved into the study and sat in chairs before the fire. It was June, but still cool outside and a fire took the chill out of the room.

"William, I want to sincerely apologize to you for the way I treated you when you were little. I was a terrible mother. I deprived you of a comfortable, peaceful childhood and I am truly sorry for that. There is no excuse for the way I treated you. You were a human being and deserved to be treated with respect and dignity, even when you were an infant. I did not do that," explained Anna.

"Why? Why did you treat me like that?" asked William.

"At first, probably because I was scared. I did not want to be pregnant and never wanted to have a child. When Will left me in Astoria, he promised me that he would be back in 3 months. Your grandfather sent his friends Isaac and Julia Sorenson to Astoria to take me back to Portland. I did not want to go, but Isaac went to the shipping lines office and found out that it could be up to one or two years before the ship got back to Astoria. The man at the office seemed to indicate to Mr. Sorenson that Will knew that it would be that long. He abandoned me in Astoria living in a rooming house and working in a dirty diner on the docks. I didn't even have the money I had made on the boat from Rawlings to Astoria. He took that too. I was afraid, but determined to make it on my own. Mr. and Mrs. Sorenson finally convinced me that they could leave a message at the shipping office that would let Will know where I was."

"When we got to Portland, I realized that I was pregnant and that scared me even more. I was not ready to be a mother and had never wanted to have a child. Because I was acting so badly, your grandparents came to Astoria to get me and take me home. Neither one of them knew that I was pregnant until they got to Portland. It was a difficult time for all of us. Your birth was not an easy one, mostly because I would not cooperate with the doctor or your grandmother."

"I did not want to take care of you in any way, but your grandmother forced me to. I learned to change your diaper, feed you and do what was necessary to keep you comfortable but that was all. I did not hold or cuddle you like a mother should and I tried to get you out of my mind when I wasn't around you," Anna tried to explain.

"I still don't understand why you would not care for your own child," William stated rather forcefully.

"I guess it is very hard for me to explain to you. When I was young, I resented anything or anyone that would take attention away from me. I wanted the best of everything; the best dresses, the best hair ribbons, the best toys, and I wanted everyone's attention all of the time. I thought I wanted everything. I resented it every time Mama had another baby. That baby would take attention away from me. I was so mean to Aunt Susan when she was pregnant with Jeffrey. I wanted all of her attention too. At Christmas, I hated the fact that my sisters and brother would get presents as nice as mine. When you were born, I knew that your presence would take Mama and Papa's attention away from me and I hated that idea. I wanted them to belong to me and no one else. I don't know what caused me to feel that way. I just always wanted to be number one in everyone's mind and I knew that when you were born, I would no longer be number one. Actually, I was only number one until your Aunt

Irene was born," Anna stated emphatically. "And I believe that is what started my problems. I was not number one anymore. I'm surprised that I realized it because I was so young, but I knew that this other person was taking my Mama and Papa away from me. And with each successive addition to the family, it got worse. I let it get worse in my mind," added Anna.

"How did you finally figure that out in your mind Anna? What turned your thinking around?" asked Susan.

"William, when the idea of giving up custody of you was first talked about, I resisted. I was not going to let anyone take away something that belonged to me. But I finally realized that it was inevitable that you would be given to Steven and Jane. When I went back to Lewiston without you, at first I was angry, but I gradually realized that life was easier for me. Now I would not have another person to be responsible for and I could get all of the attention again. There were no sisters or brothers, aunts, uncles or cousins or child to take the attention away from me," Anna explained. "But you know, it did not happen the way I thought it would. People still didn't pay any more attention to me than they did before. I was still only the bartender at the lounge in the Lewiston Hotel. I had some dates, but they were never really serious and I knew that I did not ever want to get married again, so I finally stopped accepting any requests for dates. Anna said emphatically.

"What did you want?" asked Jeff.

"I wanted respect!" stated Anna. "I wanted people to respect me for myself and for what I could contribute, and I realized that being a bartender was not a job that garnered a lot of respect. That is when I thought about going to school."

William sat there in Jeff and Susan's study mesmerized by what his mother was saying. He had never thought about the fact that there was a reason for the way she treated him.

"So, if I hadn't been born, you would have been okay?" asked William.

"No, William. Never think that. Even though it was rough for a lot of years, I am glad you were born. You are a fine young man and Steven and Jane have done an outstanding job of raising you. I guess I have not been doing such a good job of explaining myself and my actions. There was, maybe still is, some sort of defect in my system. I am now convinced that no one caused this defect, it was just there. My parents did the best job they could raising five children. I can't imagine ever doing something like they did. I know that they gave us everything that they could and both of them always gave us an abundance of love. Unfortunately, I was never able to give it back to anyone. I thought I could to your father, William, but I know now that that would not have worked either," Anna emphasized.

"I guess now, my biggest task is to learn how to love. I need to learn to love and trust others as well as myself," said Anna. "By the way, how is your dog?" Anna asked.

William perked up when Anna mentioned Patch. "He is great! He's outside running and playing with the other dogs. He loves to be here on the ranch because he can run and not have to be fenced into the yard. Patch is the best friend anyone could ever have," William stated. "What are you going to do now?"

"I will go back to Lewiston for a short time and then I think I will take the train to Portland and go visit your grandparents on the coast. I have also been doing a lot of reading in the past year and have the urge to see the Ocean like my Papa did. I also need to see my parents in person so I can try and make amends to them also," explained Anna. "I must get going now and get back to town. Jeff, do you have someone who can drive me back?" asked Anna.

"Certainly. Let me go get him," answered Jeff.

"William, thank you for listening to me today. I hope that someday, you will at least understand my actions and that we can be friends," Anna said with a tear running down her face.

As the buggy pulled up in front of the house, Susan opened the front door to let Anna out. "Thank you, Susan," said Anna quietly. Susan put her arm around Anna and gave her a quick hug. William stood in the background just watching his mother leave, not knowing what to think of the whole situation.

As Anna was being driven back into town, she made the decision to catch the train the next day and go back to Lewiston. She would gather her things together, quit her job at the lounge and then catch the train to Portland. From there, she would go on to the beach and see her parents. She had talked to the rest of her family and now she needed to see her parents. There was not much she could do about her brother and sister's feelings about her now. She had said her piece and she felt relieved that it was over. At least no one threw rotten tomatoes at her, she thought, chuckling to herself.

Irene opened the door for her when she heard the buggy drive up and immediately questioned how the afternoon went.

"How was everything? Was William there? Did he listen to you?" asked Irene in quick succession.

"Fine, yes and yes," answered Anna with a smile on her face. "William was there and he did listen. I am not sure how much he understood, but I was totally honest with him as to how I felt when he was born and how I feel now. I let him know that he was in Rawlings to stay, that I am not capable of taking care of another person. I hope he understood what I was telling him. He was very quiet and I am sure he will have many questions to ask Steven and Jane after I leave. I tried to explain to him the best that I could."

"What are you going to do now?" Thomas asked.

"I am taking the train back to Lewiston tomorrow morning. Then I am going to quit my job, pack up my belongings and go to Portland. I will contact Mama and Papa and hopefully go see them. I have a lot to explain to them and I really want to see them," answered Anna.

"Why don't you send them a wire and let them know you are coming," said Irene. "It might make them feel a little more prepared for your visit," said Irene.

"I will do that. Thank you so much for letting me stay here with you. You have a lovely home and I appreciate you hosting the family for dinner. I hope that what I said will help repair some of the damage that I did to all of them. Even though we will probably never be close to each other, I would like to be considered a member of the family. I really didn't know how much I missed everyone until you were all gone," Anna said quietly.

Steven and Jane rode out to the ranch to see William after they knew Anna had left town. They were concerned about how he felt and whether he wanted to leave with his mother or not. They had no idea what Anna had said to him, so were unaware of his feelings.

William was out on the range with Daniel and Seth when Jane and Steven arrived at the ranch. Cora answered the door and let them in. Both Susan and Jeff were in the study going over the books for the month and were surprised when Steven and Jane walked in.

"Well, hello! What brings you out here?" asked Jeff.

"We couldn't wait to hear about Anna's visit with William," answered Jane. Does he want to go back to Lewiston with her?"

"No, he doesn't. He wants to stay here with you. He is confused about her and her attitude towards him, but he does know that he does not want to leave

Rawlings," answered Susan. "He will be fine. He just needs to process what his mother told him. I imagine it is hard for him to hear that he was not wanted, but I also know that he is a very smart young man and knows that he is wanted by all of us."

"We will head for home now. I really don't want William to think that we are checking up on him," said Steven.

"Won't you stay for supper? William will be glad to see you," said Susan.

"Thank you but no. We are supposed to meet Charlotte for dinner at the hotel. She is going back to Spokane tomorrow," said Steven.

Jane gave Susan a hug as she left the house. "Thanks for being such a good sister. I love you lots!" said Jane.

Chapter 15

William stayed at the ranch for most of the summer. He was enjoying being with Daniel and Seth and the rest of the ranch hands. Jeff and Susan let him stay in the bunkhouse with them and eat his meals with them. The hands were advised not to let him do anything dangerous. He was not as skilled as the other cowboys. He was a good rider and was confident on a horse but did not have the experience to do a lot of the jobs that the cowboys had to do.

It was time to round up the young calves and brand them with the JSJ Brand. It was not a fun job for most of the cowboys, but a necessary one. William had asked if he could help with the branding. Earl was hesitant about letting him help and asked Jeff what he thought.

"He is young and inexperienced, but if he is going to be on the ranch and wants to help, maybe we should let him participate," said Jeff. "He is a smart kid and knows what happens when you brand. Let him be there, ask Seth and Daniel to watch him. If he gets the least bit green, get him out of there. I don't want him to be turned off by any of the work that needs to be done on the ranch."

Earl noticed that William was totally engrossed in what he was doing, to the exclusion of anything else. If he was not helping with the branding, he was practicing roping. He was using a fence post as a target and, according to both Seth and Daniel was doing a pretty good job of hitting the target. He had a good eye and good aim.

Anna's visit was put to the back of people's minds as daily life continued in Rawlings. The ranch was continually busy in the summer with all of the chores that needed to be done in the good weather.

Great excitement was in the air when Clyde and James decided to install a gasoline pump and tank. The pump was on order and Clyde and James had decided to put it just to the side of the store. That would leave the front available for customers to come in easily, but also give the drivers of cars easy access to the gasoline pump.

Blake and Fiona Stephens were the first ones to order a motor vehicle. Blake thought it would be a better way to visit his patients on the outlying farms. But it would be several months before it was delivered. Henry Ford was developing a car that was enclosed. Blake felt that one of the open cars that were available now would not work for him in the farm country with all of the dust and dirt.

Life continued to be busy and active in Rawlings for the remainder of the summer. School started again in September with more students than Irene had ever had. There had been three new families move into the area during the summer and they all had school age children. There were 22 students in 12 different grades and the classroom was packed. A couple of extra tables and some chairs were donated to the school by Freddie Seevers. He had extra tables and chairs stored at the hotel. He had ordered some new ones for the dining room and had not disposed of the old ones yet.

The Mayor, Ray Clausen called for an emergency city council meeting to address the crowded school situation. He proposed building an addition on the school to provide a separate room for the high school students. He also proposed hiring another teacher giving Irene the choice of teaching the grade level she wanted to teach. The council members all agreed that a new school and teacher were necessary but were concerned about how they were going to pay for them.

"It seems to me that the only way we can pay for a new classroom and teacher is by raising taxes and we are already asking our citizens to pay for the roads with the taxes that they pay. How can we ask for more?" asked Bill Kingman.

"Clyde Rodgers is installing a gasoline pump at the store and Doc Stephens has already ordered a car. Granted, they will not be delivered for a while, but a tax will be added to every gallon of gasoline sold to be used for maintenance of the roads. I firmly believe that once Doc Stephens' car arrives, others will be ordering them for themselves. I know I probably will. It will be a much easier way to make the rounds of the farms to do my work," Ray explained to the council members.

There was much discussion about the tax increase and finally Ray asked for a vote. There would be two issues to vote on. The first, the increase in taxes to pay for a new classroom and teacher for the school and the second to actually build the addition and hire another teacher. The council voted "yes" on both proposals. They all knew that it was necessary to have additional room at the school and an additional teacher.

Irene and Thomas were advised of the councils decision the next day. Irene was relieved that she would not have to be responsible for the education of 22 students in 12 different grades all by herself. Ray had asked her to contact the district superintendent in Dayton about securing a new teacher.

"Ray, I would prefer to teach the older students, so I will request a teacher for the younger students. I think it will be easier to attract a younger teacher that will be willing to live here. Most of the older teachers I have met want to live in the larger cities," said Irene.

"Whatever you think is best, Irene," answered Ray. I appreciate you handling this for me."

Irene sent a letter off to the superintendent of public instruction in Dayton requesting applicants for an elementary school teacher. She explained the situation at the school and that they were in the process of building an additional room for the high school students.

Within three weeks of sending the letter to the school superintendent, Irene had 3 letters from prospective teachers. Two of the letters were from older men looking for teaching jobs to finish out their careers. Both of the letters were almost exactly the same, indicating their requirements for strict discipline and their propensity towards corporal punishment if they were not obeyed. Irene rejected the letters on sight. The third letter was from a 20-year-old woman who had taught in Missoula, Montana for 2 years. She sent along references from her co-workers and the administration of the school where she was working. They were all excellent references. She said that her reason for leaving the school was the size of the school and the size of the town of Missoula. She wanted to live in a small town. She said she was raised in a small farming town in Eastern Montana and wanted to get back to that type of living.

Irene wrote her back saying that she was very interested in meeting her. She also explained that she would have to be certified by the State of Washington, but because of her references, she didn't think that would be a problem. After several letters back and forth, Irene asked Susan to review the letters and give her opinion about hiring Alice Beacham as the new elementary school teacher for the Rawlings school.

"Boy, with those references and her experience working with other teachers, I would hire her in a flash. The fact that she wants to live in a small farming town is a big plus for us. She will not be as inclined to leave as quickly as someone who wants a big city," exclaimed Susan.

"That's what I felt, but I wanted your opinion as well," added Irene.

Irene let Ray know what was happening as far as the new teacher was concerned. He was very pleased with the results of Irene's search.

"We will probably be ready for the new teacher after the first of the year. The addition should be completed by that time. Jeff and Susan have donated the money for additional desks and chairs for the new room and they should be delivered within a month," Ray said.

It looked like everything was ready to go with the new classroom. Irene was just waiting for Alice Beacham to arrive to take over the elementary students.

When the train arrived with Doctor Stephen's car, the town turned out in force to see it taken off of the rail car. It was a beautiful black machine that looked, to a lot of the people, like it would be very complicated to drive.

Once it was off of the rail car, Doc Stephens got behind the wheel. He got out again and asked a bunch of the fellows standing around to help him push it to the store so he could put some gasoline in it to get it started. Ford Motor Company had sent him an instruction book ahead of delivery so he would be familiar with the workings of the car. Blake had read a lot about motor cars since he had ordered his and knew that he had to turn a crank at the front of the car to get it started, but it had to have gasoline before the crank would work.

Clyde ran ahead of the crowd so he would be ready to pump the fuel into the car.

"Just put a gallon in this time Clyde," said Blake. "I want to see how far it will go on a gallon of gas."

After Clyde put the gallon of gas into the tank and Blake paid him for it, Blake started the car. After a couple of attempts, it started and Blake drove back to the clinic. The townspeople ran along side of the car and cheered him on. It was a new experience for all of them.

Ray had made a space in the stable for the doctor to park his car out of the weather, but every time he started it up, the noise spooked the horses and it was hard to calm them down.

"Doc, we are going to have to make other arrangements for your car. The stable is not a good place to park it. The horses are spooked every time you start it and the fumes of the gasoline are probaby not good for them," stated Ray.

"I will park it behind the clinic for now and put a cover over it. I didn't even think about the noise bothering the horses. I'll check with Earl Jansen about building some kind of lean-to to park it under," answered Blake.

A lean-to was built behind the clinic and the car no longer disturbed the horses in the stable, but when Blake was out driving, if he passed a horse, the noise of the car made the horses skittish. They didn't like it at all and a lot of the residents didn't appreciate the noise either. There were complaints to the mayor and other members of the city council about the noise and the fact that it was dangerous to ride a horse into town when the motorcar was in use.

Ray and the city council decided to call a town meeting about the use of motor cars in the city. Several people in town had ordered cars and Ray knew that the noise level would only increase with the additional cars on the roads. He felt the problem needed to be addressed as soon as possible with the citizens of the city.

The meeting was called for the first week in March. The weather had eased up some and the streets were muddy, but passable.

"Thanks everyone for coming tonight. We obviously have a problem that needs to be talked about. The noise level has gone up since the doctor has been driving his car around town," explained Ray.

"It sure has!" someone yelled from the back of the room. "I can hardly ride my horse into town when Doc is out driving."

"I understand it is a problem for a lot of you, but we are going to have to get used to the additional noise. There are going to be more cars on the road in the near future and several of you farmers have ordered gasoline powered vehicles for use on your farms and ranches. It is the way of the future," Ray explained.

"May I speak?" asked Doctor Stephens. "I want to let you know that I try very hard to only use my car for visits to the farms and ranches to treat you people. When I have a home visit in town, I walk as I always have. When I am out at one of your homes and I have to transport one of you into the clinic to treat you, it is much quicker and easier to use the car. I have space in there and it keeps you out of the weather during transportation. I am really sorry for the additional noise, but I was only thinking of your welfare and my ability to treat you all quickly when I decided to order the vehicle."

The room quieted down somewhat after the doctor explained his use of the car. Some of the other residents spoke up about their feelings on the car, but the consensus of most of them was that this was the way of progress and they were going to have to get used to it.

One of the town residents said, "We got used to the train noise and whistles day and night, I guess we can get used to the noise of cars on the road."

Alice Beacham was settling into her job as the new elementary school teacher at the Rawlings school. The children loved her and Irene enjoyed working with her. They had very few projects together, but occasionally would schedule a joint activity.

Alice had been living in the hotel since her arrival in January and was beginning to think that she needed a place to settle down. She couldn't afford to buy a house, but wanted to rent something small with a kitchen where she could fix her own meals. She liked the food in the dining room but wanted to try her hand at cooking for herself. She also wanted to be able to invite people to her home instead of always going to theirs.

Alice had become friends with Freddie Seevers, the manager of the hotel and he said that he would help her look for a place of her own.

"Alice, answer your door!" Freddie called as he knocked on her hotel room door one Saturday morning. Alice stumbled to the door, putting her robe on quickly.

"What is wrong? Is there a fire?" cried Alice.

"No, not an emergency, but I just heard of a little house for rent about a mile from the school house and I thought you might like to see it before anyone else does," explained Freddie.

"What time is it?" asked Alice.

"It's 8:00 o'clock in the morning," said Freddie.

"Good grief! It's the middle of the night," exclaimed Alice. " I sleep later on the weekends. Give me a few minutes to wake up and dress. Yes, I would like to see the place. I will be ready in 20 minutes. Please meet me in the dining room so I can at least get a cup of coffee before we go."

"Ok! I will even buy you breakfast when we get back." Freddie answered.

It was a pretty April day when Freddie and Alice drove out to the little house on the hill that was for rent. The owners had died and their children were not ready to sell the house and property yet. They decided to rent it out for a time before they made their decision.

Alice closed her door and laughed at how excited Freddie was. She thought that he was a nice guy and was pleased that he was looking out for her. She washed up, put some clothes on and combed her hair. After she applied some lip gloss, got her coat, and walked out of her room towards the stairs to the dining room. Freddie was sitting at a table with two cups in front of him. When he saw her come in, he got up, got the coffee pot, and poured both of them a cup. Alice drank it gratefully and then was ready to go.

Because the weather was mild, they decided to walk up the hill to the house. Alice was impressed with the outside of the house. It was white with blue trim, had a flower garden in the front and what looked like the remains of last year's vegetable garden at the side of the house. A white three board fence went around the entire property with a gate in front and a gate at the side of the house.

The inside of the house had all of the furnishings still in place, including dishes, silver service and pots and pans. There was a good wood stove in the kitchen and a water pump at the kitchen sink. There was an indoor bathroom in the hallway and a small bedroom with a single bed in it. A small closet was available in the bedroom to hang clothes.

Alice was impressed with the house and wanted it right away, but it was a little more rent than she expected to pay. Unfortunately there was nothing else available within a reasonable distance to the school and the city center. She decided that she would talk to her folks and see if she could pay them a little less per month on the money she owed them.

After making a long-distance call from the hotel to her parents, she told Freddie that she was going to rent the house they saw that morning. Thomas Campbell was handling the rental transaction for the owners so Freddie and Alice went to see him. Thomas was delighted that Alice wanted to take the property and informed her that if she ever wanted to buy the property, the money that she was paying towards rent would apply to the down payment on the property.

"That is a very good opportunity and I thank you for telling me. The thought of buying property is a little daunting to me at this time, but I will consider the offer.

Thank you for handling this rental for me. I am looking forward to moving in. From the looks of the house, all I will have to buy is food. Everything else is there, even a full wood box," said Alice.

Freddie helped Alice move her things from the hotel to her new home that afternoon. All she had was her suitcase with her clothes and several boxes of books.

"Why do schoolteachers have so many books?" Freddie asked. "My Aunt Susan was a schoolteacher and she has a whole room in the house at the JSJ Ranch devoted to her books and my sister Irene has a whole wall of books in her house."

"We are committed to reading and teaching our students to love reading. Only by having the books available and having read them ourselves, can we instill the love of reading into our students," explained Alice. "Books can take us on adventures that we may never be able to go on in person. I have been able to travel all over the world through stories in books."

"My Papa was a great reader. He learned in an orphanage when he was very young and has read everything he could get his hands on since then. When he was young, he read a story about Lewis and Clark being at the Pacific Ocean and Papa's biggest dream was to see the Pacific Ocean," said Freddie.

"Did he ever get to see the ocean?" asked Alice.

"Yes! He and Mama live in Cannon Beach, Oregon. They both love it there," answered Freddie.

After putting her clothes and personal things away, Freddie brought in her boxes of books. There was no place to put her books. One bookcase in the living room was already full.

"Just put those boxes over in the corner and I will sort through them when I have time. I need to get down to the store now and stock up on some necessary food items," said Alice.

"I will take you in the buggy. You will have a hard time walking back up the hill carrying grocery bags," offered Freddie.

"You have done so much for me already. I shouldn't impose on your time. You have a hotel to run," said Alice.

"I don't mind at all. I signed myself out for the day. Believe it or not, I took a day off," Freddie said with a chuckle.

"Okay, I appreciate the assistance. Let me get the grocery bags that I found in the kitchen," said Alice.

Alice and Freddie took the buggy to the store so that they could easily get her purchases home. Alice had an idea of what she wanted to buy. She found everything on her list and found that the store had some fresh early season vegetables displayed in front of the store. She picked up some early season lettuce and some green peas. She was excited to make her first meal in her new home. James asked her where she was going to keep all of these groceries and she told him about renting the house on the hill. James looked at her strangely and told her that he was thinking about renting that place himself.

"I live with my mother and Clyde in the apartment above the store and was thinking it was about time I get a place of my own," James explained.

"I am sorry! I rented it the other day and moved in today," explained Alice. "I am sure another place will become available soon."

Freddie took Alice back to her place. She thanked him for his assistance in the move and said goodnight to him at the gate to her yard. Freddie was disappointed that he was not invited in but said goodbye to Alice and left to go back to the hotel and his lonely room. He was definitely interested in the new schoolteacher.

Chapter 16

Freddie Seevers was busy running the hotel. He tried to be involved in all aspects of the hotel business. Steven was teaching him the ins and outs of ordering supplies for the hotel. Steven's accounting business was growing and he found that it was difficult for him to do all of the ordering of supplies for the hotel, dining room and general store on a timely basis. James Kingman was doing a good job of learning to order supplies for the store. He only had to seek Steven's advice occasionally now. Freddie wanted to get to the same place in his ability to order supplies. Ordering supplies for the restaurant was fairly easy. Jim Barnes, the chef ordered his own food supplies. He knew exactly what he wanted and tried to serve only fresh food in season, so it was easy to get. Clyde and James were able to supply him with any other supplies that he needed. The Indians were very good about bringing in fresh wild game. Beef, pork and chicken were supplied by farmers in the area.

Freddie loved the hotel business. When he was little, he spent a lot of time in the lobby talking to the guests. He still did that. He tried to welcome every new guest to the hotel and make them feel comfortable. He would help carry luggage to rooms and make sure that the guest was comfortable and had everything they wanted.

Freddie's father had been the chef in the restaurant and he did not have the time to interact with the guests. When he was training Freddie in the hotel business, he stressed the need to make the guests feel at home and Freddie took it to heart.

Freddie was a tall, good-looking man. He was pampered by his sisters and parents because he was the only boy, but he was not spoiled. He was a very good student and did well in school. He had thought he would like to go on to school and take some classes in business, but money was not available for his schooling and he really did not want to leave Rawlings.

School was out at the end of May 1909 and most of the students went to work on the farms and ranches in the area. Some of the older students who lived in the city thought it would be fun to take Doctor Stephens' motorcar out for a ride. Late one evening, four of them gathered behind the clinic and pushed his car out of the lean-to where it was parked. The boys pushed it out onto the road just beyond the hotel, turned the crank to get the car started and off they went down the road. They made the mistake of driving the car right by the sheriff's office. John Boyson, the sheriff of Rawlings happened to be awake and sitting in his office doing some paperwork at the time the noisy car went by. He looked out the window and noticed that it was not Doctor Stephens driving the vehicle, but four boys having a great time weaving all over the road. He stepped out of his office and into the middle of the street.

"Are you boys going someplace?" the sheriff yelled over the noise of the car.

Three of them jumped out of the car and started running, but they ran right into Doctor Stephens, who was walking out from between two buildings.

"Why are you running boys?" asked the doctor.

All three boys stopped abruptly, then hung their heads and said nothing. Blake turned them all around and walked them back to his car and the sheriff.

"We just wanted to see what it would be like to drive a car," one of the boys said. "We didn't do any harm to the car," cried another boy.

"When you take something that does not belong to you, it is called theft. The penalties for theft are more severe the higher the value of the stollen item. A car costs a lot of money. The penalty for theft of a car is pretty severe. I am not sure what Doctor Stephens wants to do, but for tonight, all four of you are going to jail. I will notify your parents as to where you are so they will not worry when you don't come home until morning. Unfortunately, your parents probably will have to pay some money to get you out of jail.

All four of the boys were begging the sheriff not to tell their parents, but it did no good.

"They weren't too smart, were they sheriff?" Blake said. "You can hear this car all over the city. The minute they turned the crank, I heard it back in the clinic."

Sheriff Boysen led all four of the boys into the jail, put them in the two available cells and locked the doors.

The next morning, the town was in an uproar about the events of the night before and that four of their high school boys had spent the night in jail. Steven and Jane were very glad that William was at the ranch. All four of the boys were friends of his and he might have been with them had he been in town. Some of the people thought it was funny that the boys had stolen Doctor Stephens' car. They figured that boys would be boys. They thought it was not necessary to put them in jail though. It was just a simple prank. Others felt it was a silly thing for them to do, but that they shouldn't have been locked up for the night. Then there were the ones who were horrified that the good Christian boys would steal anything at all and what were their parents thinking, letting them be out on the street at that time of night.

The theft of Doctor Stephen's car was the main topic of conversation in the restaurant and at the general store that morning. It was also the main topic of conversation among the parents of the boys. A couple of them were hard pressed to come up with the $3.00 it cost to bail them out of jail. All four couples were very angry at their sons for pulling such a stupid stunt and grateful to the sheriff for taking care of it. They were sure that nothing like that would happen again.

"I believe that there needs to be some consequence for your actions besides spending the night in jail and putting such a burden on your parents," the sheriff lectured the boys. "I have talked to the mayor and city council members this morning and we feel that some sort of community service needs to be done. Therefore, we have decided that since the clinic badly needs to be scrubbed down and painted on the outside, that would be a good job for you boys. You will be working individually on the project so no two of you will be together. The rest of the time, you will be out picking up trash, sweeping porches and walks in front of the businesses and doing any other odd jobs around the city to make it look better. You have one month to finish the painting project. After that one month, if the job is done to the satisfaction of Doctor Stephens, your record will be cleared. If it is not done to his satisfaction, you will continue until it is. Do you have any questions?" Sheriff Boyson asked.

"No sir!" came the answer from all four boys.

The town of Rawlings eventually got back to normal after the car theft. The four boys involved did a great job painting the clinic. It looked like new and Doctor Stephens deemed the job complete after six weeks of work. All of the businesses enjoyed having their porches swept daily and the town was never so clean as it was when the boys finished picking up all of the litter. Picking up all of the litter also included cleaning up after the horses. The ladies felt much more comfortable walking across the streets without all of the horse droppings to step over.

William spent a lot of the summer at the ranch with Seth and Daniel. He felt very comfortable around them and liked working on the ranch. He did spend some time in town with Steven and Jane. They missed having him with them but understood his desire to be at the ranch.

One day Jeff approached William about the work he was doing on the ranch. "William, I am going to start paying you for the work you are doing. You work just as hard as some of the cowboys do and you should receive a fair wage for that work."

"Thank you Uncle Jeff, but I just like doing the work because it is fun," answered William.

"I'm glad you are having fun working with the boys, but you are also helping me a lot and deserve to be paid for the work that you do. I will pay you $6.00 per week. I can't pay you the same as the other hands, but I think it is a fair wage for the work you do," Jeff stated.

"Thank you!" said William as he beamed at his uncle.

After receiving two paychecks from Jeff, William was elated with the amount of money he had. He had never had money before and didn't know what to do with it. Jeff suggested that he talk to his Uncle Steven about what to do with his money.

The next time William was in town with Steven and Jane, he talked to Steven about where he could hide his money.

"I think it would be a good idea if we go over to the bank and talk to Mr. Sorenson about what you should do," said Steven.

"Hello Jacob," Steven said as he and William walked into the bank. "How are things?"

"Can't complain, Steven. Business is good. People around here are beginning to trust putting their money into the bank. What can I do for you today?" Jacob said.

"William has been working at the JSJ Ranch for some time now and Jeff has started paying him for the work he does. He has saved some money and wants to know what to do with it. I figured you are the best one to advise him," answered Steven.

"What kind of work are you doing out there William?" asked Jacob.

"I ride with Seth and Daniel Kingman and check fences, round up strays and am learning to do some branding," answered William. "Uncle Jeff has started paying me $6.00 a week for the work I do, but I don't know what to do with it."

"You know, both Seth and Daniel have savings accounts here at the bank. They are very good about saving their money," explained Jacob.

"Mr. Sorenson, could I open a savings account here?" asked William. "I only have $12.00 saved."

"You certainly can and that is a very good start to a savings account. If you continue to save your money, you will have quite a nest-egg by the time you are ready to go to college," explained Jacob. "Let me take you over to my wife Emily and she will help you complete the paperwork needed to set up the account."

"Thanks Jacob! I did not want to force him to save his money, but I didn't want him to spend it all either. I didn't have to worry about this with the twins.

They went right from high school back to college in the East and never had a job," explained Steven.

"How are the boys doing?" asked Jacob. "I miss seeing them around town."

"We do too! We hear from them about once a month. They each write us a letter. I am hoping that when they finish their residencies, they will be able to make a trip home. It has been six years since we have seen them and that is far too long," said Steven.

William came bounding up to Steven and Jacob with a big grin on his face. "I am finished, Uncle Steven!" he exclaimed, waving his little book around showing that he had money in the bank.

The Kingman children had heard nothing about their father for some time. Otis was back at the Walla Walla state prison and causing problems. He spent more time in solitary for infractions than he did in his regular cell. His idea of solving problems had always been fighting.

Seth, Daniel, Bill, James, Josephine, and Margaret were technically his next of kin on the prison records, but none of them wanted to hear from him and asked the prison not to let him contact them. They had no good memories of him at all.

Either Jeff or Earl made a trip into town twice a week to pick up the mail for the ranch. When they got back to the bunkhouse, they sorted the mail and distributed it accordingly. Neither Seth nor Daniel ever received any mail and were shocked one day when Jeff handed them a letter from the prison. The letter informed them that their father, Otis Kingman was killed in a fight with another inmate. They wanted to know what to do with his remains. If they did not hear from the survivors, he would be buried in the prison cemetery.

"I guess we need to inform our brothers and sisters about this," Seth told Jeff. "If it's okay with you, we can ride into town now to let them know. We have no pressing jobs to do and William is in town. Maybe he could ride back with us."

"No problem, boys. "You go ahead and do what you need to do," agreed Jeff.

The boys rode into town and tied their horses up in front of the hotel. They wanted to let their mother know the news also.

"What are you boys doing in town at this time of the day?" Virginia asked Seth and Daniel.

"We got a letter from the prison telling us that Pa was killed in a fight with another inmate. We thought we had better tell the other kids before word got around," Daniel explained to his mother. "They want to know what to do with his remains."

Virginia showed no emotion at all and said that he should be buried in the prison cemetery.

None of Otis's children showed any emotion on hearing of their father's death. Virginia called Josephine on the phone to let her know. She was working as a nurse in a hospital in Spokane.

Bill and James agreed with their brothers that their father should be buried in the prison cemetery. Margaret had very little memory of her father. Her only childhood memories of him were of being hungry and cold.

Seth and Daniel stayed in town and had supper with Clyde, Virginia, and James that evening. Nothing was mentioned about their father. That period in their life was over with his death.

William opted to stay in town for a few more days. Some of his friends were going fishing and he wanted to join them. Steven and Jane were trying to encourage him to associate with some of the other students in his class at school. They felt that he needed something to focus on besides the ranch and Seth and Daniel.

School was about ready to start in September of 1909. William would be in the tenth grade and was starting to think about what he would do after he graduated from high school. He was pretty sure she wanted to do something with agriculture and farming. He was curious about everything that went on at the ranch. He really would like to have his own ranch. Jeffrey Jr. was home from college for the summer and William knew that he would inherit the JSJ Ranch. He only had a few more classes to take before he got his degree in agriculture management.

"Uncle Steven, can I talk to you for a minute?" William asked his uncle one Saturday afternoon.

"Sure. Let's go out in the back and sit," answered Steven.

"I want to talk to you about my future. I know that my working at the ranch is going to stop when I start school next week. I am not going to have time to be out there very much. I have been thinking about what I would do after I graduate from high school," explained William.

"You do have some time to figure that out William. You still have 2 years of high school left," commented Steven.

"I know, but the problem is, I don't get along very well with Jeffrey Jr. and I really don't think he likes having me working out there. He doesn't even listen to Earl's instructions as far as the hands are concerned. He tells the guys to do things differently from what Earl wants and assigns them different jobs. I haven't been out riding with Seth and Daniel now for two weeks. He has me mucking out the stalls and doing a lot of the really dirty jobs," explained William.

"Have you talked to Jeff about this?" asked Steven.

"No. I did not want him to think I was complaining about my job," said William. "I know that he has fired some of the cowboys who have complained about the work they had to do."

"Do you want to stay in town and not work at the ranch anymore?" asked Steven.

"No, I want to be at the ranch, but I don't think that I fit in there anymore. Even Seth and Daniel have said that things are going to get more difficult when Jeffrey Jr. takes over," explained William. "They are not sure whether Earl will stay on as foreman."

"I didn't realize things were getting that bad out there," answered Steven. "Earl has been there since Jeff established the JSJ Ranch. It would not be the same without him."

"If it is okay with you, I think I will stay in town until school starts. It is only another week. Jeffrey Jr. is going back to school next week also. He will be finished with all of his classes by the end of the term in December," said William.

"William, this is your home. You do not ever have to ask our permission to be here. Your Aunt Jane and I love having you here. We miss you when you are at the ranch. I do think that you need to find some time to talk to Jeff about your decision though," said Steven. "Why don't I ask your Aunt Jane to invite them in for dinner next weekend? It might be easier to talk to them here than at the ranch.

"Thank you Uncle Steven. That would be great," answered William.

Susan and Jeff came to town the next Saturday afternoon and stayed overnight at the hotel so they could attend church the next day. They had supper with Jane, Steven, and William on Saturday evening.

William poured out his whole story to them. He was nervous about telling them about Jeffrey Jr., but Steven encouraged him to tell the whole story, so he did.

Both Jeff and Susan were shocked at the feelings the hands had about their son. The idea that Earl would leave the ranch was unheard of. He was almost family and a part of the JSJ Ranch. They knew that there was some tension between some of the hands and Jeffrey, but they had no idea how much.

"Thank you William for telling us this. I need to know what is going on at my ranch and how the hands feel. I do not blame you for anything that has happened. Please know that. Your Aunt Susan and I love you and love having you with us at the ranch," said Jeff.

"Thank you Uncle Jeff, but I think I will stay here now and get ready for school to start. There are a couple of books that I want to read before school starts and I don't have as much time to read when I am at your place," William explained to him.

"Thanks for the supper, Jane," Susan said as they hugged each other before leaving. "We'll see you tomorrow morning at church. We probably won't stay in town after church. We have a lot to think about and a lot to talk about and it is best that it be done at the ranch."

After Jeff and Susan left, William asked his Uncle Steven, "Do you really think I did the right thing telling them all that? They looked pretty hurt!"

"You did the right thing. As Jeff said, he needs to know what is happening on his own ranch, especially if it effects his son and his foreman," answered Steven. "Don't worry! I also think you made the right decision to stay in town until school starts. You do not need to be in the middle of problems out there."

Chapter 17

Within the next two weeks, three more motor cars were taken off the rail cars. Jeff and Susan Jordan had ordered one, Thomas and Irene had ordered one and Bruce Williams ordered the third one. Again, the whole town came out for the unloading of the cars. Earl drove Jeff and Susan into town in the buggy so they could drive their motorcar back to the ranch. Jeff had several of the hands working on the main road to make sure that it was not badly rutted so that the car would drive over it without too much bumping.

Thomas and Irene drove their car to their home. They had a lean-to constructed next to their house to park the car.

Clyde was busy at the gas pump the day the cars arrived. All three of them needed fuel before they could be driven very far.

Bruce Williams was the last person to pick up his car. People were surprised that he had purchased a vehicle, but he had made a very good living off of the property he owned and the property he had purchased from Virginia Rodgers. He raised chickens for eggs and meat as well as raising some pigs and sheep. The sheep he raised for the wool that they produced. Bruce's wife

Marjorie spun the wool into yarn and sold it to Clyde at the general store. Many of the ladies in town loved getting the yarn to knit or crochet sweaters, hats, and scarves and socks for the winter months. It provided Clyde with a popular item to sell in his store and an additional income for the store.

School started with a blast of hot weather in September and the children were not happy about being closed up in a classroom. Alice and Irene both decided to have some outside study time with lessons about flowers and trees in the area. For a science project, Alice had her students select some different types of plant life and catalog it. The children all had fun collecting leaves and flowers from all parts of the city.

Alice had asked Freddie if she could display some of the student's projects in the lobby of the hotel. Freddie thought it was a great idea and set up some tables for her to put the displays on. Most everyone who came into the lobby on their way to the restaurant looked at the display and were impressed with the work the children had done.

Freddie would have done just about anything that Alice asked him to. He was falling in love with her very quickly and the feeling was becoming very obviously the same on Alice's part. They were together most of the time and spent their weekends riding in the country before coming back and having a meal together either at the restaurant or at Alice's home.

Freddie wrote a letter to his parents telling them all about his love for Alice and his desire to propose marriage. He wanted their blessing before he proposed.

Freddie wanted to find someone who would be a back-up manager for the hotel. If he was to be married, he didn't want to be on duty 24 hours a day like he was now, but he could think of no one in town who would qualify to work the night shift. Maybe his Aunt Irene would know if one of her graduating students would be qualified to train for the job. He really couldn't pay anyone very much, but they would have a free room and at least two meals a day. Someone who owned or ran a hotel now was said to be in the hospitality business. It took someone with a special personality to do a good job. He would ask Irene for a recommendation.

On a Saturday afternoon in late September when the weather was still mild, Freddie took Alice on a buggy ride down towards the river. He had a picnic lunch in the back of the buggy and a diamond ring in his pocket and he was very nervous.

"Let's spread our blanket out in this clearing, Alice," Freddie suggested. "I have brought one of Jim's great picnic lunches for us."

"Thanks, Freddie. This place is great. It is so pretty out here today. A picnic is a great idea," said Alice.

"Jim Barnes is a great cook and does a super job on putting together a picnic lunch," said Freddie.

They both sat down and spread out the food in front of them. Freddie was fidgeting around with the food. He presented the box to Alice so she could take what she wanted, but he did not put anything on his plate.

"Aren't you going to eat Freddie?" asked Alice.

"Oh, yes. I forgot to put something on my plate," Freddie mumbled. "Listen, I need to talk to you! I have something to say and I don't quite know how to say it, so I will just blurt it out. Will you marry me?" Freddie asked with an eager tone in his voice.

"Uh—I was not expecting this," answered Alice.

"I'm sorry. Maybe I am expecting too much. I thought that maybe you had some feelings for me. Maybe I am overstepping, but I am in love with you and I want to spend the rest of my life with you. I want to spend my life making you happy and having children with you and growing old with you," Freddie added.

"Yes, I will marry you. I am in love with you too and would be very proud to be your wife and the mother of your children," said Alice with tears in her eyes.

Freddie stood up and pulled the ring out of his pocket. He gave his hand to Alice to help her up. He put a beautiful solitaire diamond ring on the third finger of her left hand and gave her a proper hug and kiss to seal the engagement. Both of them had tears in their eyes and were laughing at the same time. The beautiful picnic lunch that Jim had put together was pretty much ignored.

William was excited to start school this year. He realized that he only had two years before he went to college and he had some big decisions to make about what he was going to do and where he was going to school. He was interested in agriculture and had fun working on the ranch and learning about farming, but he was also interested in the law.

"Uncle Thomas, when did you decide to go to law school?" William asked one day when he was visiting Thomas at his office.

"When I was in the 12th grade, a lawyer came to talk to us at school and he was so sincere about what he was doing and the people he was helping that it inspired me. I started reading about the law and the courts. It was something that fascinated me and I thought that I might like to look into being a lawyer," answered Thomas. "Are you thinking about going to law school after college?"

"I have been thinking about it but I don't know where I would go. I know I have to have a four-year degree before I can go to law school. Do I have to go to the same school where the law school is?" asked William.

"No. You can get your degree and then go to any law school that you choose. You do have to have really good grades though to get into law school," said Thomas.

"I remember when we went to court when my mother gave up custody of me. You were my hero for a long time because you didn't make me go back to Lewiston with her," William told Thomas.

"That wasn't me, William. It was Judge Corbin who made that decision. Unless there is a jury trial, it is the Judge who makes the decision after he hears all of the testimony. The lawyer is the one who presents the evidence to the judge or jury," explained Thomas. You have some time to make your decision. Study hard this year and do some research about the law. You can make your decision after you know more about it."

The next week, Thomas and Steven had lunch together. Thomas related his conversation with William to Steven. Steven knew that William was thinking about his future but did not know that he was thinking about the law as a career. He thought he might want to pursue a career in agriculture, but after his talk about Jeffrey Jr., Steven was not so sure. He was glad William had confided in Thomas.

Jeff and Susan were not sure what they were going to do about Jeffrey Jr. Jeff was angry and frustrated that his son was causing discord among the ranch hands.

"I think we need to have a meeting with Earl to get his take on the situation," Jeff told Susan.

"Okay, why don't you invite him up to dinner. Jeffrey has left for school, so he won't be here to intimidate Earl," said Susan.

"It's sad when you realize that your son, whom you love with all of your heart, is intimidating people, especially ones that he has known all of his life and have treated him like their own family. It hurts my heart to think that my son would do that," Jeff stated firmly.

Susan had tears in her eyes when she said, "my heart is broken over this and Jeffrey's attitude towards our employees. He treats them like they are servants and I do not know where he formed this attitude. He certainly didn't get it from us. Our employees are our family."

Jeff took a crying Susan into his arms to comfort her. "You go wash your beautiful face my sweet, and I will go down and talk to Earl about coming to dinner tomorrow evening. I'll let Cora know that he will be here and that we will want a private dinner with him."

Cora fixed a very nice beef stew and crusty bread dinner for Susan, Jeff, and Earl the next evening.

"Thanks for inviting me to dinner. I also wanted to have a meeting with you two," said Earl.

"Earl, let us go first please," asked Jeff. "First of all, we have heard about the disrespectful way that Jeffrey Jr. treated you while he was home this summer. Both Susan and I want to apologize for that. He had no right to treat you or any of the other employees on this ranch in that manner."

"Earl, we treasure you and your friendship. It means the world to us," Susan said.

"I want you both to know that both of you have become my family. I do not want to lose that, but I have been thinking about moving on. Unfortunately, with Jeffrey Jr. working here, I will not be able to stay. He and I do not agree on the way chores need to be done on the ranch," explained Earl. "I tried to explain to him that the foreman of a ranch is the one who assigns the jobs to the cowboys, but he informed me that since he was the owner of the ranch, he was the one who would assign the jobs."

"Well, he is not the owner of the ranch. Susan and I are the owners and we will remain that way for many years. He might be the son of the owners, but that is all. He has no say in the operations of this ranch and if he is not careful, he never will have any say," Jeff announced very angrily.

Earl sat there somewhat stunned by what Jeff had said. It was hard for him to believe that anyone would disinherit his child.

"We will not accept any disrespect on this ranch. We are trying to run a business. It is hard enough dealing with the weather, the animals and their health and everything else that comes up on a daily basis without having to deal with infighting among the employees. That includes our son," stated Susan. "Unfortunately, he forced William away for the last couple of weeks before school started and William is family."

"Since you have opened up about Jeffrey Jr., I am going to relate some of the things that the boys have told me," Earl said. "Apparently, Jeffrey does not believe that William is family. He called him an outsider and he wasn't to be trusted because of his father. I heard him talking to some of the hands in the bunkhouse one afternoon that Seth and Daniel could not be trusted either because their father was in prison and they would probably end up there also. Unfortunately, I think some of them believed him because they started excluding Seth, Daniel, and William from any of their activities."

Susan hung her head and had tears rolling down her face.

"I am sorry Susan. I do not like to make anyone feel bad, but I know you need to know this. I did not want to come forward earlier. I did not want you to think I was complaining and did not know what your attitude would be towards your son running the ranch. But some of the boys have come to me privately, saying that they think either Seth or Daniel have stolen from them. They have been missing personal items, belt buckles, little bits of money, and other odds and ends. One of the fellows was missing his good pair of boots."

"I cannot believe either Seth or Daniel would steal from anyone. They suffered terribly because of their father and hated the way he treated them and their brothers, sisters, and mother. This ranch has been their home since they were teenagers. They learned to read and write and began to learn the love of reading here. They would come into the study and sit and read in the evenings after they had a long day working. They are honest and good men now and deserve respect for what they have accomplished, not scorn for their beginnings," stated Susan angrily.

"I agree and I tried to explain that to Jeffrey Jr., but he only said that I was just an employee and didn't know any better. I shut my mouth then and said very little more to him. I only talked to him when I had to," Earl added. "It wasn't very long before he returned to school."

"Susan and I have decided that we are going to make a trip over to Pullman to talk to him in person. He probably won't like what we are going to say and we have had to make some hard decisions, but we have decided he will not inherit the ranch. We will not disinherit him completely, but he will not have the ownership of the ranch nor will he have anything to do with the running of it. We are going to have Thomas draw up new wills for both of us saying that Seth and

Daniel will inherit the ownership of the ranch equally. With your continued help, we feel that they will do an outstanding job of running the JSJ. In time, we will let the rest of the hands know about our decision. I guess we have to take a little time for ourselves."

Earl was astounded at their decision but privately, very pleased. He would not have stayed on with Jeffrey Jr. running the place.

Jeff and Susan took the train to Colfax, stayed the night and the next morning boarded the train for Pullman. They were both apprehensive about talking to Jeffrey, but knew it had to be done. They did not want to lose their only child and were heartbroken at the idea but could not tolerate his attitude towards their friends and employees.

Jeffrey Jr. was not expecting a visit from his parents and was not at home when they arrived. They checked in at the local hotel and called him. Jeffrey had an apartment just off of the campus and had his own phone. When he answered, Jeff heard a lot of noise in the background.

"Hello Jeffrey! Your mother and I are in town and would like to see you. Will you join us for dinner at the hotel this evening?" asked Jeff.

"Sorry Pop! I have made other plans. If you would have let me know you were coming, I could have made some time for you, but I am tied up for a few days with classes and studying," Jeffrey said, slurring some of his words.

There was a lot of noise in the background and someone yelling for Jeffrey to get off of the phone. Someone called Mary was waiting for him.

"I'm sorry to hear that Jeffrey but make some time. We have come all this way to see you. And that is not a request Jeffrey. Do it!" commanded Jeff.

Jeffrey slammed down the phone and went back to his drunken party.

Jeff was livid when he hung up the phone. He walked back up to their room and told Susan what had happened. "We have his address and it is not far from here. We will walk over in the morning and see what kind of condition he is in. He was drinking and had several people at his place. There was someone named Mary waiting for him," Jeff said, frustrated at the position he and Susan were in.

"Oh Lord! What are we getting into?" asked Susan.

"We shall see!" answered Jeff.

The next morning, as they were walking to Jeffrey's apartment, both of them were very quiet, not knowing what to expect when they got there. Jeff knocked on the door several times and there was no answer. Finally, he banged on the door with his fist and some strange girl answered the door. She only had her underwear on but was not embarrassed to stand there in front of Jeff and Susan.

"What you want?" she slurred. "It's too damn early for someone to be banging on the door."

"Where is Jeffrey?" asked Jeff.

"Who wants to know?" she asked with a surly voice.

"His parents want to know. The people who pay for this apartment want to know," Jeff relayed to the surly girl.

The girl turned around and yelled, "Jeff, your old man is here. He wants to see you." Then she left and went into another room.

Jeff came stumbling out of another room putting a robe over his naked body. "What the hell are you doing here at this hour?" he yelled at his parents.

"You get everyone out of here now!" commanded Jeff.

"I can't do that. This is my apartment and I have whoever I want here," Jeffrey yelled at his parents.

"Go get dressed and tell everyone to leave NOW!" commanded Jeff.

Jeffrey turned around and stomped towards his room like a little boy. Susan almost laughed because that was what he did when he was a little boy and was chastised for something.

Slowly, the eight other people there gathered their things together and left, grumbling all of the way out the door. Susan went into a very messy kitchen, found some coffee and the dirty coffee pot, washed the pot and three coffee cups. She stoked up a very small fire in the stove and put some coffee on while Jeffrey was dressing and the others were leaving. She couldn't imagine anyone working in such a dirty surrounding. She decided not to clean it up however. That was Jeffrey's job and he had to learn to take responsibility for his own actions.

"Sit down, if you can find a place in all this rubble," Jeff ordered. "Your mother is making some coffee. I imagine you need it right about now."

"I want to know what you are doing barging into my apartment without an invitation," asked Jeff.

"First of all, Jeffrey. This is not your apartment. It is mine. I have paid the rent on this place for three years. I paid for your food, your clothes, and apparently your liquor. I have paid your tuition for four years of college and I have given you a substantial allowance for your incidental needs. So, with that fact in mind, do not say that this is your apartment. I am letting you live here on a month-by-month basis. Let me tell you, my patience with you is pretty thin right now, so you had better watch what you say to your mother and me," Jeff asserted.

Susan came out of the kitchen carrying three cups of coffee and handed one to each Jeff and Jeffrey. Jeffrey took his gratefully and took a long drink of it, almost spitting it out because it was hot and very strong.

"Good grief Mom, what did you do, put the whole container of coffee into the pot," Jeffrey sputtered.

"Well Jeffrey, I figured you probably needed it extra strong to sober up this morning," answered Susan rather sarcastically.

"This is too strong. I can't drink it," said Jeffrey.

"Drink it Jeffrey!" demanded his father. "You are going to need to be fortified for what we are going to say."

Jeffrey looked at them with wide eyes, wondering what he did wrong. He had no idea.

Jeff proceeded to tell him just exactly what he did wrong. He listed the infractions one by one.

"If I ever hear of you being disrespectful to Earl or anyone of the workers on the ranch, you are out of there. You will not be welcome back," stated Jeff firmly. "Your mother and I are going to see Thomas when we return home and have our wills changed. We are leaving the JSJ Ranch to Seth and Daniel Kingman. Upon our deaths, they will own the entire spread."

Jeffrey jumped up, spilling hot coffee on his leg and on the floor. "You can't do that!" he yelled. "I am your son and the heir to the JSJ Ranch. It is my inheritance!"

"Not anymore! You have abused the privilege of owning that ranch. We will leave you an inheritance which will be enough to get you started on any business you want, but you will have nothing to do with the ranch," stated Jeff firmly.

Susan sat there with tears building up in her eyes. She was trying to figure out what went wrong. Maybe it was because she taught him at home. He didn't have a lot of association with other children his age. Maybe it was because he was an only child and they spoiled him. He always had almost anything he wanted. She knew that he always resented the attention that Patch got when William brought him to the ranch. All of the hands loved him and played with him. They did not play with any of Jeffrey's dogs. His dogs were not loved and cared for like Patch was. You could tell by the attitude they had when they were around humans. They growled and sometime bared their teeth. The ranch hands pretty much left them alone.

"Now, get yourself dressed and clean this place up. It is a mess! We will be back in an hour and take you someplace for breakfast," said Jeff.

"No thanks! If you are going to disinherit me I want nothing to do with you. I realize that I am dependent on you financially right now, but I will get a job as soon as I can so I will not be asking you for more money. I will be out of your apartment as soon as I can find another place to live."

"Jeffrey, that is not necessary. You can stay here until you graduate," said Susan.

"I probably should tell you this now, but I will not be graduating. I dropped out of school at the end of the last term. My grades weren't that good anyway," admitted Jeffrey.

"And you didn't see fit to tell us this?" asked Jeff. "What did you do with the tuition money we sent?"

"I spent it! It was fun having extra money for myself," Jeffrey asserted. "Now, why don't you leave and let me figure out what I am to do with the rest of my life. I might even get a lawyer and sue you for parental support and neglect if you continue with this crazy idea of yours of disinheriting me. I have planned my life around owning that ranch."

Jeff and Susan just stood there in shock at what Jeffrey was saying. Neither of them could figure out what had happened to their boy.

"I guess he will figure out quickly what to do with the rest of his life when there is no more money coming from Mom and Dad," said Jeff very quietly as they walked out of the apartment and back to their hotel. They gathered their things together, took a buggy to the train depot and took the early train back to Rawlings. It was a long two-day trip to get home and they barely spoke the whole time. They just held onto each other.

Life proceeded fairly quietly for Jeff and Susan when they returned to Rawlings after their ill-fated trip to Pullman. The day after they got home, they went into town to see Thomas. Both of them had a difficult time telling Thomas their story and their plans.

"Are your sure that this is what you want to do?" asked Thomas. "He is your son!"

"We know! We have talked about this until there is no more talk in us and we agree that right now, he doesn't deserve to own or run the ranch. He is ill-equipped and emotionally unable to maintain a healthy relationship with the employees and to make the decisions necessary to keep the ranch in good condition. We are afraid he will run it into the ground in a year," explained Jeff.

"Both Seth and Daniel are much more capable of keeping the ranch growing. They have lived and worked there since they were in their early teens and they know every inch of the land. It is sad to say, but we trust them so much more than we do our son," added Susan.

"Okay. We will add a codicil to your existing will naming Seth Kingman and Daniel Kingman owners of the JSJ Ranch upon your death. It will also say that you will bequeath Jeffrey Jordan Jr. the sum of $10,000 to use as he sees fit. Is that what you both want?" asked Thomas.

Both Susan and Jeff answered with a "Yes" at the same time.

After the Jordan's left Thomas' office, they went to visit Virginia. She was home at the time and Clyde was with her. James was working downstairs in the store and Clyde had taken some time off.

"Well, hello you two!" Clyde said in surprise as he opened the door to Jeff and Susan. "Please come in. Virginia, we have company," he hollered to his wife.

"We are sorry for barging in like this, but we have something important to tell you," explained Susan.

As Virginia came out of the kitchen, she asked, "Are the boys all right?"

"Oh yes! We didn't mean to scare you," answered Susan.

Jeff proceeded to tell Virginia and Clyde the story of what had happened to Jeffrey, Jr. and what they were planning to do with the ranch.

Virginia had tears running down her face. "You have truly rescued my boys. There is no way that I can ever repay you for what you have done for them. You both have been more their parents than I have," she said.

"No! You will always and forever be their Mama. They love and respect you as their Mama. Please know that. We were able to physically give them a place to live and work. We have grown to love and admire them both and trust them enough to give them our ranch, but you will always be the parent. Probably the most difficult and most important thing you ever did as their parent was to give them up to us. We thank you for that," Jeff added.

After the Jordans left the Rodgers, James filled their motorcar with fuel and they drove back to the ranch, knowing that they had done the right thing. They still had to tell Seth and Daniel what they had done but would hold off on that for a while. They would ask Earl to quietly work with them and teach them what needed to be done to be owners of a large ranch.

Virginia was stunned by what Jeff and Susan had told her. She couldn't believe that all of her children were in good places now. With the terrible way that their life started and the abuse that Otis piled onto them, she doubted if their lives would ever be normal. But her two oldest boys had their future set for them, Bill was supremely happy with this farm, Valerie, and little Ginny. James was set with the running of the general store. He was looking for a place of his own and growing into a fine man. Josephine was an accomplished surgical nurse at Sacred Heart Hospital in Spokane and Margaret was ready to graduate from high school and wanted to go to Lewis Clark Normal School in Lewiston to become a teacher. And her life with Clyde couldn't have been better. They were as much in love today as they were the day they were married. Virginia was grateful to God every day for her life and the lives of her children.

The 1909 – 1910 school year went by fast and William did very well in his studies. His grades were excellent and his family was very proud of him. He spent the summer of 1910 at the ranch working with Seth and Daniel. William still didn't know that his friends would inherit the ranch someday. He did know that Jeffrey Jr. had not graduated from college and was not coming home for the summer. He didn't know why but didn't really care. Without him there, life was easier for all of them. William did realize that both Uncle Jeff and Aunt Susan were much quieter and spent more time with each other than they used to. Jeff made the major decisions about the ranch but left everything else up to Earl. He also noticed that Seth and Daniel seemed to have more responsibility than before but decided not to say anything or ask any questions. He was just happy to be with them.

With the help of Steven, Jane, Thomas and Irene, William had made the decision to apply to the University of Washington in Seattle and work towards a pre-law degree. If he liked Seattle, he would probably stay in the area for law school. He was ecstatic when he received his acceptance letter to he University. It was the start of a whole new life. He was content with the life he was mapping out for himself and with the help of his family, was a very happy young man. When he saw his friends with their fathers, he regretted never knowing his father and the relationship with his mother was pretty non-existent, but maybe someday. He had this whole, large family who loved and supported him.

Steven and Jane were going to take some time off when William graduated and take a trip with him to Cannon Beach, Oregon to visit his grandparents.

He would probably see his mother at the same time. She worked for an attorney in Seaside, Oregon. After that visit, they would take Steven to college in Seattle.

After a rough beginning, William's life had turned out pretty well. He had started out his life in Rawlings as a scared, weak little boy. Now he was a strong young man ready for life to begin and ready to take on any challenge that came before him. Life was good!

Printed in the USA
CPSIA information can be obtained
at www.ICGtesting.com
LVHW021349040924
790081LV00001B/79